Other Books

By Chad Morris & Shelly Brown

Mustaches for Maddie

Squint

Willa and the Whale

By Chad Morris

*The Inventor's Secret:
Cragbridge Hall, Book 1*

*The Avatar Battle:
Cragbridge Hall, Book 2*

*The Impossible Race:
Cragbridge Hall, Book 3*

By Shelly Brown

Ghostsitter

VIRTUALLY ME

CHAD MORRIS AND SHELLY BROWN

SHADOW
MOUNTAIN
PUBLISHING

To all the amazing teachers and students
at Sam Morgan Elementary, Fairfield Junior High,
Davis High School, and throughout the world who
made the best of school during the pandemic!

Interior illustrations by Garth Bruner

Visit us at shadowmountain.com

Library of Congress Cataloging-in-Publication Data
(CIP data on file)
ISBN 978-1-63993-053-1

Printed in the United States of America
Lake Book Manufacturing, Inc., Melrose Park, IL

10 9 8 7 6 5 4 3 2 1

CHAPTER 1

NOT
TOILET PAPER

Bradley

I definitely didn't expect the FedEx guy to change my life.

Summer was dying, showing all of those I'm-about-to-end signs, like the cheesy back-to-school-with-a-brand-new-look commercials, or stores loading up whole aisles with notebooks and binders. All of my summer plans had already happened, not that I did much. Nobody did too much during the pandemic, but I probably did less than they had. My mom had splurged and bought me a new pair of jeans and a bag of socks. I know, super exciting stuff. I could feel my freedom ticking away so I was dealing with it in the most mature way possible: sitting in my pajamas in my dad's recliner, eating Kix, and bingeing YouTube videos.

Mostly K-pop music videos.

But also some movie trailers.

And a clip where a toddler tried to eat an ice cream cone, lost his balance, and totally face-planted onto the whole cone. So funny and cute. But sad. But also really funny.

And a baby duck that followed a dog.

And then some more K-pop videos.

It was noon. Don't judge me. I was mourning my imminent loss of free time and independence.

But at least the music was daebak. (That's a Korean word that means "awesome.") In the last music video I'd watched, seven girls sang in Korean then bopped into this catchy chorus in English, "Sweet like peaches, strong like steel, want to be with you forever, this love is real." K-pop helped me through some tough parts of last year. Not only is it amazingly well done, it's also so positive. It lifted me when not much else did. My favorite group is the Bubble Girls and my ultimate bias is Sooni. The girl has serious moves. I'm an official Boba (Bubble Girls fan) and an unofficial Tumbler (Avalanche fan.) My absolute favorite part of K-pop is the dancing. Incredible.

Sometimes I wish I could be in a K-pop group, or a boy band, or whatever, but I'm more a solo artist. Of course, that's not necessarily by choice. Not sure who I would be able to convince to sing and dance with me; I can't even get people to sit with me at lunch.

I swayed in my chair. I might be the best chair dancer ever. Later, I'll get up and completely go for it. I'm a big kid—you could say fat. I do. But I can follow their moves, especially Avalanche. Sometimes I dance for a few hours at a time; it's not like I've got anything else to do. I'm a pretty good dancer. At least I think I am. And my mom thinks so too. But it's not like anyone outside my house would ever see me. You don't ever see enough people my size in music videos. But maybe someday, when the pandemic goes away, I could go on one of those huge talent shows on TV, and then the meanest of the judges would roll his eyes when he saw me, and the nicest judge would give me a chance. And then the music would come on, and I'd start to move—and everything would change. There would be like a moment of total surprise, because I'm not just good, I'm amazing—then the crowd would go crazy. And I'd get a standing ovation, and one of the judges would slam the button that brings down all the glittery floating things from the ceiling, and I'd be famous overnight. And all the kids from my school would wonder how they hadn't even realized I exist when I'm that totally awesome.

Or maybe they'd slam the button that would release a se-cret trap door that would drop me into the I-can't-believe-you-thought-you-had-talent pit of embarrassment. And the video clip of me would go viral and everyone would laugh and wonder how I ever thought I was good.

That was more likely. I should probably just stick to dancing in my room.

Knock.

Thunk.

Those two familiar sounds outside my door could only mean one thing—delivery time. It was probably toilet paper.

My mom orders all the boring stuff for our house online. She did it even before the pandemic made it cool. Our laundry deter-gent and shampoo are just dropped off in boxes at our front door.

And my parents weren't here to get it. Even in a pandemic, my dad had to manage the food factory, and my mom had to help in the plumbers' office. I was going to wait to get it until I'd finished this video, but then I imagined someone stealing a box of toilet paper off our doormat. (Toilet paper porch pirates are the lowest of criminals.) So I rolled out of the recliner, being careful not to spill what was left of my Kix.

Opening the door, I noticed that this box was orange and shimmery instead of the classic brown cardboard.

Unexpected. And maybe a sign that it might be better than toilet paper.

The box was a long rectangle the size of two shoe boxes end to end. As I carried it inside the apartment, I noticed it was lighter than liquid laundry detergent but heavier than . . . Cheetos.

I was hoping it might be Cheetos anyways. Maybe they were really packed in there.

The name on the label caught my eye. It wasn't for my mom or dad. It was for me—Bradley Horvath.

So weird. I never got packages. My parents would have had to let me use their credit card, and that wasn't happening. Too late for my birthday, too soon for Christmas.

Please be Cheetos. Please be Cheetos.

I didn't really have any money to order K-pop posters or merch or anything, so this was new. A hundred guesses of what it could be raced through my mind. Maybe somehow my mom figured out I really want to dye my hair pink like Park Hyun Min, the rapper in Avalanche. Or maybe it was an amazing camera to film my moves. (Not that I was ready to show them to anyone.) Or maybe I have a secret admirer out there who wanted to send me a surprise gift. Lol. A boy can dream. Or maybe I won a contest and inside was like a million dollars and plane tickets to go see the Bubble Girls in Seoul.

I just really hoped this orange shimmery box wasn't full of toilet paper.

Carrying the package to the kitchen counter I noticed that the label had a return address—Balderstein School District—and my heart sank like the toy car I'd accidentally dropped in Stuart's pond when I was five. This package definitely didn't have hair dye, an amazing camera, or concert tickets. It was school stuff.

Cue the sad trombone.

But maybe it was something different than regular school stuff. A few months ago, my mom had asked me if I wanted to try the district's new online school. She said a lot about it being a new opportunity, and that with the pandemic the school district was trying new things, giving students more options. But I'd said "yes" at the word *online*. We had to do several weeks online at the end of last year when the pandemic shut down schools. I think most people hated it—not me. School in my pajama pants with no people around? Yes, please.

I full-on *hated* regular school. I hated it worse than when my parents canceled Netflix because I watched it too much. (Thankfully, it's back.) Worse than having to wait for a book in a series I'm reading to come to the library. Worse than when the Wi-Fi goes out. Worse than sitting in a stinky house after someone heats up fish in the microwave. (Yeah, that one was low, but school deserves it.)

Especially after the incident at our third-grade program in front of the whole school. Even though that was more than three years ago, and I'd moved on to middle school, I still heard people whispering about it and saw them pointing at me. I was the kid they thought peed his pants while singing "America the Beautiful." But I hadn't—stupid Shawn Undergate shot me with a squirt gun just before I stood up at the mic. And his friends took pics. (Yeah, there were evil conspiring third-graders with phones waiting for just the right moment. And those pics are still out there. I've seen them.) I've never been able to clear my name.

I was either the kid who peed his pants, or people had no idea who I was. Some kids might talk to me when they're new or lonely, but eventually I'm either just a laughingstock or a no-body—either infamous or invisible. Which is probably why my one-man dance show isn't happening any time soon.

No matter what, I didn't have to go back to middle school. Our middle school was for fifth and sixth grades, and I was start-ing seventh, so I'd be moving on to junior high. I hoped there would be kids from all over the district at the online school so I could start fresh.

Grabbing a butter knife I cut through the tape on the pack-age, slicing it like an experienced surgeon.

I pulled back the flaps, trying to figure out what an online school would need to send me. A laptop or something? But the shape wasn't right—the box was too narrow for that.

Just under the flaps was a letter. "Blah, blah, blah," I said and set the letter aside. Who reads the paper first? Besides, I knew what it was going to say:

Bradley Horvath,
Thank you for choosing to save us money

by going to an invisible school. Because of your mediocre grades and unremarkable social status in middle school we wanted to give you this box of candy and K-pop posters. We hope it makes up for the horrible pit of shallowness that was middle school and puts you in a better mood to start junior high, which we expect to be just as boring as middle school but with less social anxiety. Or maybe more.

All the best, or worst, or whatever—we don't care,

The Administration (who might be real people or maybe bots)

PS The next box has Cheetos.

I ripped out the bubble wrap, not even bothering to pop any of them—I'd save that for later.

I stared at something that blew my mind into a trillion pieces, put it back together, and then shattered it again.

There was a lot my mom hadn't told me.

CHAPTER 2

COOLER
THAN CHEETOS

Bradley

Goggles. Sleek and shiny.

But not like stupid ski goggles, or "flying debris" woodshop goggles, or I-can-see-you-underwater swimming goggles.

Virtual reality goggles. Like the kind I keep begging for for Christmas or my birthday or Groundhog Day or the groundhog's birthday—or any day the groundhog or anyone else wanted to give them to me.

And not just normal VR goggles like you could buy at the store. These were incredible. They had the attached surround-sound headphones and face-tracking cameras. They had temperature-control fans. They had a boom microphone.

My nerdy heart pounded like the beat to Avalanche's hit "Show Stopper."

I lifted the goggles out of the box like they were the crown jewels. Or some ancient precious vase in a crate at the museum. Or the last donut in the box when I knew I wouldn't get another

8

donut for a month. Or like I was the last kid I knew who didn't have a VR system.

So daebak.

I put them on and pushed the power button. The interface cushions that rested against my face were as soft as marshmallows, but thankfully not as sticky. That would be incredibly unsanitary.

Darkness.

Oh, right! I needed to charge them. Without power they were just a fancy blindfold.

While they charged, I turned back to the package. Under another layer of bubble wrap I found two controller gloves, then a tracker belt and ankle straps so the computer would know how my body was moving. A normal VR system only comes with the headset and handheld controllers. This was like a bonus package with all the (expensive) extras.

After I charged it all, I put it on, feeling a lot like an action hero gearing up for the final showdown against the forces of evil. (Seriously, when you tighten that many straps, you just have to say things like "gear up" while imagining the movie montage.)

As I put on the goggles, my world changed immediately. I wasn't in my room anymore. I was in a school hallway lined with lockers. I was somewhere else entirely.

I mean, I *know* that's what VR does, but it wasn't like I'd ever had friends that invited me over to try out their system.

It was both awesome and terrible at the same time. The graphics were amazing, but the location was completely disappointing. *School? Seriously?* Why not walking the Great Wall of

China, or landing on Mars, or on a concert stage in front of millions of fans?

A woman stepped out of one of the classrooms into the hallway just a few feet in front of me. Her avatar was stylistic, a mix between a photo and a video-game character. She was tall with light brown skin, a blue dress suit, and one of those short bob haircuts that look really professional and also kind of like a grown-up Dora the Explorer.

"Welcome to Balderstein Virtual Junior High," she said. "I'm Mila Holota, the director of the virtual school department at NovaMillennium, the company that made this virtual school. She spread her arms out, gesturing around. "As you can tell, Balderstein VJH will look similar to a regular school in many ways." She was right, though it was a bit larger and looked completely clean, which made it unlike any school in the Balderstein District that I'd ever been in.

Dora the Explorer Lady continued. "It will have hallways, classrooms—" She stepped into a classroom and my point of view followed her without me doing anything. I was on some sort of automatic tour. There were desks and a whiteboard wall. "—and a gym." Like cutting from one movie scene to another, my point of view followed her into a large gymnasium with basketball hoops and bleachers. "Because our company also makes virtual games, you will have access to some of them as well. For example, Balderstein VJH includes a rec room." We moved into a large room surrounded by various games. There were bowling lanes, a mini-golf course, and basketball hoops with nets between and beneath them to bring the ball back to the shooter. I'd never seen that in a school before, but it did make some sort of sense. If we were already in a virtual world, it probably didn't take much to include some games.

"You will have plenty of time to explore the school and the rec room at our orientation party. I'll tell you more about that later."

Orientation party? I didn't like the sound of that. I wanted to explore these games alone. Just me. Only Bradley. Bradley Solo. The Lone Brad. A party meant people, and that had words like *awkward, uncomfortable, painful,* and *people-you-don't-know-whispering-about-you* written all over it.

I hoped it was optional. I'd rather stay home.

"But first," Dora Lady held up a finger, "you—" she said, pointing at me. (Okay, I'm sure she was pointing at anyone wearing the goggles as they watched the introduction, but right then it was me.) "—you need to make your avatar. Upload several pictures of yourself from different angles. Our program can use it to make a realistic avatar. That's what I have done." She twisted a little to the left and right, modeling her own avatar. It was pretty cool that they could do that. I mean, I'd seen all the YouTube videos of people using filters to turn themselves into cartoons or cats or even game avatars, so the technology has been around, but I hadn't ever done it.

"We recommend you use the real-life photo filter," Dora Lady said. "Just be you." She pointed at me again. "Wonderful you." She obviously didn't *really* know who she was pointing at. I hated the way I looked. I wasn't ugly or anything—at least I didn't think so. But I wasn't good-looking either. Nobody was wishing they had my round body or boring brown hair and eyes. I was just super forgettable . . . unless you've seen that picture of third-grade me with wet pants.

"However," she continued, "it's also possible for you to customize your avatar. But that must be approved by a parent or guardian *and* your homeroom teacher before orientation. Please submit it before the sixteenth of this month."

Customize?

That word hung in my brain.

Customize.

It was like it echoed the second time with more meaning. Like I could change things about myself? Like maybe *so many* things that I could change *all* of me? Like I could walk the halls and no one would whisper about the third-grade incident.

Customize.

I almost didn't even dare think it, because I was afraid it wouldn't be true.

But I thought it again.

And again.

Maybe I didn't *have* to be me.

The idea was catchier than the chorus to a Bubble Girls song.

It even made me a little emotional. (Not a lot emotional; I saved that for the last episode of a really good series.) A tiny bit of moisture *might* have escaped my eye, though.

I knocked my hand against the goggles as I reached up to wipe the tear.

Note to self—don't cry in your VR equipment. It's really awkward.

CHAPTER 3

A MODEL IN AN ASTRONAUT HELMET

Edelsabeth

"Edelsabeth," my mom called out from the other room, "have you finished yet?"

I love my mom. She's probably my favorite person in the universe; no offense to my dad or little sister. It's just Mom gets me in ways I don't think anyone else does.

But not right now.

I'm furious with her right now.

If my feelings were a person, they would be rocking a fiery crimson dress, red hair teased out in every direction, insanely thick eye makeup, stomping around in steel-toed patent leather boots. Oooh—and add a pitchfork that shoots lightning.

"I'm still working my magic," I said in a singsong voice, trying to keep my cool.

"I still working magic too," three-year-old Eva's voice mimicked from behind me.

How long had she been there? With these dorky goggles on I

could have accidentally stepped on her; I'm basically blind. *And* she could be finding and destroying anything in my room. She's really good at that. "Out of my room, please, Eva," I said, trying not to let my anger with Mom spill over at her.

"But I'm magic," she said. I lifted the goggles to see her dancing around my room, cupping one hand next to her eyes like they were holding goggles, the other hand pretending to wield a magic wand. "And you're a . . . kangaroo," she said, waving her pretend wand at me.

Cute but crazy.

I have to admit she did help my mood a little. Three-year-olds can be good at that too.

"Sorry, Eva," I said. "Time to go."

"Not without my kangaroo," she said.

"You could turn something in your room into a sparkling unicorn with wings!" I said, making it sound exciting. "That's even better."

She gasped. "Good idea."

I heard her tiny feet patter across the carpet and out the door.

I slid the goggles back on and got back to work. Adjusting the virtual clothes on my avatar, I was surprised with how good it looked. The pictures I'd uploaded caught the waves of my long dark hair, the size of my eyes and lips, and even my makeup. It wasn't perfect, but for a digital version, it was impressive.

"Can your magic work any faster?" Mom asked, sounding much closer, like she was in my doorway. Her voice was sweet, like she wasn't being evil and making me switch schools again. My dad agreed to it too, but we all knew it was Mom's idea.

When we moved from Houston last year I'd switched schools, and I'd worked hard and made a lot of friends. But now all of them would be going to real school while I stayed home with these weird goggles on my face. And with the pandemic, it wasn't like friends could just hang out after school all the time. They would forget about me.

What kind of parents made you miss real life with your friends? That's like telling a kid to spend *more* time on their phone.

"You've been on that program for two hours," Mom said. "This is worse than you getting ready in the morning."

"Now you sound like Dad," I said.

If it had been that long, it was her fault. She was the one who never thought my avatars were good enough. She'd even made me retake the pictures I'd submitted. This was my third try.

Normally I'd just draw the clothes I designed on a notepad or my phone, but this was a whole new level. If I had to go to some terrible virtual school, completely alone, I was going with style. I had to make a great first impression. But each time I designed the perfect look, Mom said it was too much. Too much. Too much. What did that even *mean*?

The first attempt, I'd made myself everything I wished I was. My avatar wore a stylish light-blue crop top with a white skirt just long enough to pass school regulations. My tan skin was a nice contrast to the light colors. I'd altered my avatar a little too. I couldn't resist. I made myself a little taller, with a better figure, shortened my forehead, and tweaked my nose. And my hair was longer, with just the right highlights and curls.

When Mom saw it, she freaked out. She didn't yell or lose her temper or anything, she just told me to change it in her I'm-not-putting-up-with-this-nonsense voice. Not only was I switching schools, but she had to control my look too.

I changed it. I took new pictures, toned down my makeup and hair from a New-York-fashion-week look to a posting-when-you-look-pretty feel. I went with a puff-sleeved short dress, but then I found a setting that could make my eyelashes thick like when I use falsies, so I added that.

And she wasn't okay with it again.

So this time, I'd taken pictures with my makeup and hair the way they'd be if I was just going to school on a normal day. And I designed my clothes simpler: jeans and a white T-shirt with a lacy overlay, girl's cut of course, and I left it right at my waist. I barely even changed my avatar's forehead, nose, lashes, and figure. There was no way Mom would notice. I even wore white ballerina flats. So basic.

I didn't want to have to do this again.

I took a deep breath, took off the goggles, and handed them to Mom.

When she put them on, she looked kind of like a model in an astronaut helmet.

I guess an astronaut helmet wasn't entirely right. The VR goggles only covered her eyes but had straps that pressed her nor-mally perfect hair down in some places and made it poke out in odd ways in other places. It was a strange accessory to my mom's black-and-white striped midi-dress.

I let out a snicker.

"What?" Mom asked. "Is it because I look crazy in these goggles?" She waited for a response, but I didn't want to admit anything. "You should have seen yourself."

I felt the top of my head and instantly knew I looked like an unkempt llama. Thank heavens nobody was around to get a picture. That kind of stuff can haunt a person.

But I resisted the urge to run to the bathroom to fix it. I had to stay and get final approval.

My mom tilted her head up and down, examining my work.

She was taking too long. She'd *have* to be okay with it. I'd done the bare minimum to still have some style, to still be me, and feel confident enough to meet new people and make friends.

After only a few more seconds, she took off the goggles and sighed. "Absolutely not," she said, her tone still nice, but her message was not. "There is no way you are going to school like this."

CHAPTER 4

NOT PLASTIC

Edelsabeth

"Are you *kidding* me? What's wrong with it?" I asked.

"It's really well-designed," Mom said, some of her hair still askew. "You're talented. But it's still just too much." She shook her head. "Thirteen-year-olds aren't like that, Edelsabeth, and shouldn't try to look that way. You're a person, not plastic. Not a magazine cover. Not photoshop."

"That's just me, but in pixels," I defended.

"No," Mom said, "you still made changes."

"Just a few," I said, not able to deny it. "But I think my avatar's cute."

"Oh, she's very cute," Mom said—and she seemed sincere, but she also had that sass in her voice that let me know that more was coming. "But *cute* isn't the way to measure anything important."

"I don't know if that's true," I said. "Clothes, puppies, otters holding hands," I counted them off on my fingers, "baby seals, boys."

Mom just looked at me, her mouth wrinkled up. She tried to hand the goggles back. "Simplify. Everything. Again."

All that work. And how could I go any simpler? "I don't—" I interrupted, pushing the goggles away. "Mom, I really don't want to."

"If you'd rather, I can do it," Mom said, her voice growing firmer. "We talked about this. You're beautiful the way you are. You don't need to submit fashion-show pictures. You don't need all the right angles. Just make it simple, like you're hanging out at home on a Saturday morning. Maybe a little makeup and simpler clothes. It's not a catwalk; this isn't a beauty contest. You need this."

We had talked about *this* so many times. And I never liked it. I wasn't convinced.

"*You* get to look cute," I accused, pointing at her dress. I ignored her crazy hair from the goggle straps.

She looked down. "This is just what I wore to work." With the pandemic, Mom worked from home, but because she still had a lot of conference calls, she dressed up exactly like she used to.

"And this will *just* be what I wear to *school*." I gestured to the goggles she was still holding so she'd know I was talking about my avatar. "Why do *you* get to look amazing and I have to look frumpy?" Mom was trim and stylish, with long dark hair and thick black lashes. She was also Palestinian, which gave her beautiful tan skin. I'm only half, so mine is more like I spent an afternoon at the beach.

"Who says you have to look frumpy?" she asked. "I said

simple. They're not the same thing." She set the goggles on my desk. "And we aren't talking about me. We're talking about you."

I hated when she said that.

Eva came back in and pulled out the chair at my desk and sat down, whispering something about her pony. Her little three-year-old body was swallowed up in my oversized swivel chair.

"It's not just the avatar," I continued with Mom. "It's . . . virtual school. None of my friends will be there. Do you have any idea what kind of kid voluntarily signs up for virtual school? It will be—"

"Are you sure you want to finish that sentence?" Mom interrupted. With that tone, I reconsidered. "I've got an amazing seven-part lecture on the dangers of being judgmental."

"I'm not trying to be mean," I said, and I really wasn't. I was just discouraged. "I don't think I'm better than them. They just aren't the same type of kids I hang out with. We're not going to have anything in common."

Mom kept going. "Each of the seven parts of the lecture builds on the last," she said, moving her hands one over the other. "By the end, you'll be crying non-judgmental tears."

She wasn't listening to me. "Mom," I said, exasperated. "I just want to go to regular school." Even if we had to wear masks and be socially distanced and maybe even get shut down, I wanted to be there with my friends again as long as I could.

Mom looked at me for a moment then at movement from my desk chair. "Eva." She reached for my sister, who had put on my VR goggles when we weren't looking.

"I'm Edelsabeth," Eva said, trying to balance the large device on her small head. My mom pulled it off and Eva looked at me and shuddered. "It's *dark* in there."

It must have been in sleep mode, totally black.

Mom helped Eva down and gestured for me to follow her. "Let's go back to the kitchen. We'll talk it over while I make dinner."

I didn't move. Mom was a great cook. She'd start whipping up a fancy salad or kebabs, and soon we'd be laughing and chatting, and she'd talk me into whatever she wanted. "I'm just . . ." It was really hard to find the words.

She paused. "You know that I love you, but this past year has just been too much." She let out a long breath. "You need a break."

"Are you kidding me? I loved last year," I said. I'd had some of the best times of my life. I went from the new girl that everyone ignored to a trendsetter. By the end of the school year I was hanging out with Kennedy and Fetu and Hunter, the kids everyone knew. And Hunter was that guy that all of the girls liked. He was the starting wingman on the lacrosse team, and looked like he came straight out of a movie. Straight teeth, blond hair, green eyes, and a big smile. He was a big flirt too, always winking and making jokes. And I think he was especially flirty with me.

Why couldn't I just go back to school?

Mom stared at me with that you've-got-to-be-kidding-me look. Like I'd just told her something crazy, like math was the study of cats doing aerobics. "You *loved* it?"

"Yes," I said, then hesitated a little.

"Are you forgetting all the nights in tears? So. Many. Nights.

All the stress and worry?" Her voice rose. "Edelsabeth, you checked that inane website millions of times to see where you ranked. Ranked! No girls should be ranked by their looks. *No one* should." A kid named Parker had built a website where all the boys could rank how cute the girls were at our school. By the end of the year, I was consistently in the top five. Usually top three.

"It wasn't that bad," I said. "I—"

She looked around to make sure Eva wasn't nearby, then said, "I. *Hate.* That. Site." When she found out about it, she went on a total crusade to bring it down. After loads of emails and calls to administration, Parker was threatened with suspension, and the site disappeared. I was just glad people didn't find out it was my mom who'd gone all mama bear.

But then a different version of the site sprang up, and Parker denied having anything to do with it.

"It wasn't that big of a—"

"And," Mom interrupted me, raising her hand, "I'm not sure Marie Holland will *ever* forgive you."

All my words left. My heart dropped. Maybe some people make it through middle school without a big regret, but I didn't. For a split second I pictured Marie.

"I'm your mother, and I say that this *is* a big deal. I need my little girl to be happy." She paused. "Not pretty, not cute, not popular, not top-five, but *happy*. Those are not the same." She nodded to emphasize her words. "And if it takes a semester—or a year—in a virtual school to do it, we'll do it." She pointed at the goggles on my desk. "You need to make a new avatar," she said.

"Not a model. Not changed or touched up. Not trying to impress anyone. Just normal and *simple*. Just you."

"If I go any simpler," I said, "I'll be too embarrassed to tell anyone who I am."

My mom looked at me, her eyes unchanging. "I think that's exactly the problem you need to face," she said. "You will *always* be worth knowing. Always. No matter how you look."

I was about to have the worst year in school ever.

CHAPTER 5

PINK

Bradley

My mom's green smoothies had a strange texture to them that I couldn't put my finger on. You chewed them a little, kind of like peanut butter. But she didn't put peanut butter in them—so what was I chewing? And why was it green? Just one more part of my life I found unsettling.

Speaking of unsettling, orientation party anyone? Anyone?

"I'm so glad I don't work late tonight," my mom said. She was short with curly brown hair and a soft shape. She was also the office manager for Shandler's Plumbers, making appointments and reordering parts. On Wednesdays they worked late to get more business, but tonight was not Wednesday.

My dad grabbed another slice of pizza. Yep. My dinner was pizza and a smoothie—the place where my mom and dad meet. Notice I didn't say *met*. They met at a comic book convention. They *meet* by being opposites of each other. Lots of hair: no hair.

Short: tall. Carrots: donuts. Dancing: movies. Weird chewy green smoothies: pizza.

"It's homemade," Dad had said about the pizza, like he always did. He managed a department at Worthington Food Factory, a place where they made and packaged frozen food, and so for some reason, he thought he could call anything he brought home from work "homemade."

"Your orientation party thing starts in five minutes," my mom said, checking her phone. "You've got this." She gave me a double thumbs-up.

This orientation was mandatory, and since the school did a great job of communicating with parents, I was going. At least I didn't have to leave my house in real-people clothes; I would succeed or fail in my dancing pandas pajama pants.

I nodded, my insides twisting like a tornado, or a pretzel, or a really bad dancer. And something about my mom saying, "You've got this," seemed to make it worse.

I *definitely* didn't want to go. Like I wanted to get back in my dad's chair and watch videos and never leave the apartment again.

But I was also really excited to go. I mean, I had prepped for this. I had spent a long time on my avatar and he looked good. Like all caps *GOOD*. No one would recognize awkward Bradley. He was a myth, an uncomfortable tale people told centuries ago. ("Forsooth, hast thou heard the ancient tale of the unfortunate youth who sang at the festival, and his evil foe used dark magic to make it appear as though the youth had urinated in his trousers? Nay? Nor I. Methinks it was just a fabricated figment of fancy.") Thankfully my mom approved it. She knew I was really excited about it, and she thought it looked cool. I didn't really explain that I could have gone as myself, and I may have asked her right when she got home from work when she was tired and hadn't had a chance to read through any emails from the school. But she approved it.

I had a totally new look *and* a new name. And I had practiced my dance moves—just in case that was part of the party.

Half terrified. Half excited. I was an emotional minotaur or something.

My parents said tonight was "a great opportunity to make new friends." And though they say lots of nonsense like that, this time they might have actually been right; it was probably the best shot I'd had in years.

But I wanted more than that. I wanted a whole new life. I wanted to hang out with people and be invited places. (Not that I could do that much during the pandemic, but you know what I mean.) I wanted to actually get texts from someone other than my grandma—or the weekend special from the pizza place. I wanted people who were excited to see me. And maybe, if things went especially amazing, I wanted the confidence to be me. Maybe even dance a little.

If I was going to reinvent myself, I might as well go big.

And with the avatar I made, it might be the best shot ever.

But what were the chances it would work? I mean, I was still me, and my last 7,000 opportunities to make friends and change my life hadn't gone so great.

I walked into my room almost trembling. But I did something

brilliant; I put on my favorite Avalanche song and whipped out a few dance moves.

They totally helped.

At least a little.

I even shook to the beat as I put on the VR helmet, belt, and foot straps.

I put on my gloves and the screen loaded. I could shift the view to show my avatar, moving right with me to the song. He was like from-a-music-video awesome; tall, with a square jaw and my Park Hyun Min pink hair. Yep, I totally did it. And it was daebak bright. Seriously pow. My clothes mirrored a whole bunch of my other favorite artists: black leather boots, skinny jeans, a white T-shirt and a dark blue leather jacket with dangly metal things hanging from it. I honestly don't know what those are, but I thought they looked cool.

Pink hair and a jacket with dangly things. I had really gone for it. I was basically walking in like a guy that was completely invited to all of the parties. A guy who would *own* a party.

But would other people buy it? Or would they see through me completely?

I should have chosen something safer. Something more . . . normal.

Realizing my mistake, I opened up the avatar customizer so I could change it. Just a few tweaks to . . . absolutely everything.

> Your avatar has been approved and finalized.
> No changes are permitted at this time.

I was locked out and stuck with the pink hair. After our

avatars were approved, we couldn't change them unless we were only uploading photos of ourselves. And there was no way I would do that. Even then, it would have to be approved again by a parent and a teacher and there wasn't time.

There was no going back now.

Maybe that was good. Like those warriors on the documentary I saw who burned their canoes after they landed on an island they wanted to conquer. No going back. Total commitment. This is my chance to be different from what I've been. Pink-haired, jacket-with-dangly-things different. Burn-my-canoe different.

But I couldn't bring myself to enter the party. Not yet.

"Showtime," I said, and I broke out into a quick kickback and arm pump move. Maybe that would help.

I took a deep breath.

"Showtime," I repeated. This time it came out like a whisper.

And then I clicked to enter the party.

CHAPTER 6

NOT LIKE
MONSTER TRUCKS

Hunter

Doot. Doot. Doot. Doot.

I beat my chest to it.

Then it double-timed, my fists matching the pace.

Doot. Doot. Doot. Doot. Doot. Doot. Doot. Doot.

The music built, and the beat went faster. And then, just as the drop hit, I beat both my fists against my chest, and then flexed.

I didn't usually do my pregame ritual before parties, but this was different. I had to get in the right frame of mind. I had to start off strong. It would be like the start of the game. Everyone's nerves were on edge right before the whistle blew, but you've got to be ready to go at the exact right moment, not play scared or halfway.

I had already beat my heart, now I tapped my head for my mind.

Mind and heart. Go in all the way.

No one would ever guess that I would be going to VR

school. It's just not what people expect of a guy like Hunter Athanasopoulos.

But I'm full of surprises.

I reached out and opened the door with my digital hand. With the gloves, I could actually feel it a little. I guess that was part of the tech.

Really weird, but kind of cool.

The whole virtual thing was throwing me off, but at least they didn't make me ride a virtual bus to get here or anything stupid like that. I just kind of appeared in front of the entrance, and then I could lift my feet up one after the other, and my avatar would walk.

I looked like me—tall with long blond hair. I made sure to comb it right before taking the pictures for the avatar. And, of course, I was wearing my Archers Lacrosse Club jersey. Number 26. That's always my number.

I took a split second to mentally review my game plan: just be me. And if anyone asked, my mom thought virtual school would bring my grades up; like I'd do better without all the distractions of regular school and the stress of masks and whether we would get shut down and go online or not. I'd be back to regular school for lacrosse in the fall. Plus, by then the pandemic would probably be over.

No one would know the real reason I was here, and there was no way I was ever going to tell them.

I started to run my fingers through my hair, but then remembered I didn't want to. Also one of my fingers got caught on the goggles' strap.

I opened the door.

"What's up everybody?" I yelled through the room, just like I would on any first day of school. I even clapped, like it was the beginning of a game.

Start strong.

I wasn't really sure how many people heard me. The room was full of a couple hundred avatars standing and talking and playing arcade games, bowling, and shooting hoops. They even had party lights going through the place like disco balls.

"How's everybody doing?" I added, keeping the energy up.

Several avatars turned and looked at me, each a digital version of some real person. Some waved back. Some smiled, then turned back to their friends, probably wishing they had the guts to do what I do. Maybe some of them even recognized me. I mean, the school was made up of kids going into seventh grade from all over the district, but some of them had to know me.

I started making rounds through the place, saying hi to people I didn't know and giving high fives. Then I kept moving. I couldn't just be like everyone else. The whistle had blown. If I slacked now, I'd be playing catch-up later. I had to find a challenge, something that scared me, and do it.

I passed the basketball hoops and the mini golf. I could play those later. I had to push myself.

I didn't stop until I saw a girl in a yellow dress talking to her friend who was wearing a fitted black T-shirt and jeans.

Pretty girls are kind of terrifying. Seriously, they make me more nervous than a playoff game. But so many people don't talk to them and don't try to be friends with them because they're scared. I couldn't be that kind of person. So I started across the room.

My stomach was exploding with butterflies; huge ones, flapping all around. My breath wanted to go short. But I had to pretend to be confident. And I had kind of learned how. My brother Ryker taught me when I was a kid to just pretend I was confident, pretend I could do things, and a lot of the time I would surprise myself. That's how I walked up and talked to Kennedy the first time at my last school. And how I first asked Edelle to dance. They were usually ranked in the top five on Parker's website. Anytime I was around them, they had my butterflies going crazy. But by the end of the year, I was flirting with both of them every day—a little more with Edelle. She's amazing.

It also worked in the semifinals game. I was totally just pretending when I told Coach to get me the ball on the wing, and I promised him I could score. My heart had been pounding and my head filled with doubts. But I pretended I could do it, like all-in pretended, and it turned out that I could.

So despite my thudding heart and my sweaty palms, I turned to the girls.

The girl in a dress had beautiful light-brown skin, pretty black hair, and smiled a little like Edelle. Plus, her dress was dope. Not many junior high girls have a look like that. Most go more casual. Black T-shirt girl had short red hair and freckles. Both of these girls would definitely have been in the top ten on Parker's site, if not top five.

I took a deep breath. I was just about to say, "Hey, ladies. I'm

Hunter Athanasopoulos." Just confidently introduce myself out of nowhere, but it didn't happen.

Someone ran into me.

I was totally blindsided.

"Wha—?" exploded out of my mouth as I tumbled to the ground. My head spun a little because physically I was still on my feet, but my avatar had fallen. My gloves and my belt had vibrated a little to help me feel it when he hit me. I guess it kind of glitched the system.

It took me a second to realize it was just some kid who wasn't looking where he was going. He'd walked right into me. It wasn't like a lacrosse slam, or a cool monster truck collision. It was just him being spacey. He'd hit me just hard enough to knock me off balance.

I felt like a total idiot. This was my first time in this school, the first time I'd meet these girls, and I just fell over like a complete klutz, all because some kid with pink hair wasn't watching where he was going.

Seriously, he had pink hair, like neon flamingo pink. Like cotton candy, bubble gum, and lip gloss had all exploded on his head. And somehow I still hadn't seen him coming.

This wasn't me. I wasn't the kid who fell over in front of everyone. I didn't get embarrassed.

I was trying to be like I was before the stupid pandemic canceled school, and I had the worst summer in history. Trying to be the same confident kid before my problem hit, my reason for being here.

And so far, it wasn't working.

CHAPTER 7

RECOVERY

Hunter

I wanted to explode, to full on rip into this kid like Coach at halftime when our offense fell apart. I was completely putting myself out there, risking it all, and he ruined it, made me look like an idiot.

But everyone had to be watching us, and if I did that I'd look like a total jerk.

Coach Whitlock told us that we could always turn things around, even if the other team was winning. There was always a chance for a stop, a turnover, a recovery all the way back to score.

Maybe there was something else I could do.

"What happened?" I asked, getting back to my feet. It was weird because my avatar naturally got up halfway. I guess it was in the programming, because real me had never really fallen.

"I don't know," Pink Hair said. "Sorry. I wasn't watching where I was going."

I reached out my hand and pulled him up. His avatar was

halfway up as well; I just helped him the rest of the way. The gloves had tech inside them that made it feel like I was actually grabbing someone's hand.

The girls had to be watching. You can't ignore two people totally colliding into each other and falling like fools so close to you. But if the girls saw me doing something nice, that could help get me back in decent field position to start on later.

"Don't worry about it," I said to Pink Hair. I was furious inside, but I was trying to recover here. "I'm Hunter Athanasopoulos."

He gave me a look like he already knew who I was, but he didn't look familiar. Maybe he'd only heard of me. He introduced himself. He had some crazy weird name I didn't think I was ever going to remember. I really didn't get him.

But I chatted with him for a few minutes, trying to recover from this whole mess. And then I realized that I could hear the girls talking behind me. One said something about how we collided, but I helped him up, and that was cute. The other said the pink-haired kid was cute, too. Nah, that couldn't be right. But then they went back to talking about me.

Maybe this wasn't a total disaster.

I waited just a little longer, talking to Pink Hair Kid, trying to build up my confidence. My heart was really thumping. Trying to talk to these girls was hard before; talking to them after looking like an idiot was going to be even harder. This was gutsy, but this was me. I told Pink Hair Kid goodbye and just gave it a shot.

"Hey, ladies," I said. "I'm Hunter Athanasopoulos."

They smiled. "I'm Ruby," the one in the T-shirt said.

"I'm Grace," the dress girl said.

"And apparently, I'm a klutz today," I said. Not bad. Might as well just own it.

The girls laughed a little. "It was just an accident," Grace said, waving it off. "That cute pink-haired kid wasn't looking where he was going."

Good. She knew it wasn't my fault. It felt like I had been doing deadlifts of embarrassment, and I could finally drop them onto the floor.

I kind of went for it, my pulse sprinting. "I saw you two and thought you looked virtually awesome," I said. "So I wanted to come say hi." And I winked.

Winks are like a secret weapon. I think most kids would never use them. And I get it. They take a ton of courage. But if you really own them, a wink can take you from the normal-kid-next-door category to the hot-guy-from-a-movie category. Seriously. Bare minimum you're entertaining and stand out. I don't see why more people don't use them. But again, you have to really own them.

Sometimes I don't want to. I get really nervous, wondering what everyone else might think. But like it says on my poster of the Greatest of All Time dunking, "You can't be afraid to fail. It's the only way you succeed."

After my brother challenged me to do it, I winked at Sarah Marie in the fourth grade and she blushed. Then at recess she told all her friends, and they were giggling while I played football. I pretended not to notice. Part of me wanted to feel all embarrassed, but instead I just kept it up. Between plays, I turned to them, and winked again. And they all smiled and laughed and talked about me.

It's all about owning it. Once you do that, confidence is just like math or sports or whatever. Practice and it gets easier. Go after it. Don't hold back. After a little while, you can walk into a party where you know absolutely no one, scream, "What's up, people!" to everyone and walk up to the prettiest girls there and tell them they look virtually awesome.

"Want to go check out the games?" I asked.

They agreed, and I started walking through the crowd with the two prettiest girls in the room. It had been rough there for a little bit, but it felt like I pulled off a playoff win.

And a few seconds later, some cocky boy challenged me to a basketball shoot-off.

Girls watching. A little pressure. Game on.

I could still do this.

CHAPTER 8

THUNK

Bradley

Yep, a black belt in messing it up. A Jedi at being distracted. A gold-medal-winning world champion in walking right into someone else. (Yes, that means I've practiced long and hard for years and beat out all my competition throughout the globe with my awkwardness. Bow. Bow. Face-plant.)

I'd only been at the party for six minutes.

If my life was a movie, this was one of those parts that should be edited out.

I don't know why I hadn't seen him. Probably because the party was sensory overload for me. Lights were blinking everywhere— on the game machines, lasers slowly tracking around the walls, a couple of disco balls glittering. Blaring music thumped through my headphones. They weren't even picking good songs. I double-checked my audio levels. They were normal, so I lowered them.

It's really hard to reinvent yourself when all that is going on around you.

Don't get me wrong. The VR company had gone all out. The commons looked amazing. I guess when you can decorate with binary code you can make it look like you spared no expense.

And I had just seen a couple of girls find each other and hug. The thought had never crossed my mind that some people would decide to come to virtual school *with* their friends. What if everyone here already had friends? What if I was the only loner?

No. I couldn't worry about that. This was my chance.

So I tried to walk into the commons like a pop star, weaving through people like I had somewhere important to go, people to meet. And then a group of girls and a couple of boys were at my left. And I could tell they were my kind of people. I didn't want to look over too soon, because that would be weird, like I was stalking them or something. And as I walked up, it was like a slo-mo commercial. I turned my head at the exact perfect time, making eye contact with one of the girls and it was like magic. My pink hair was probably all beautiful and flowy above my casual smile. Trying to be a new me was going absolutely perf—

Thunk!

Crash!

Awkward fall into the gaping jaws of the underworld.

Or at least onto the speckled carpet. It was like I'd walked into a wall.

I didn't feel the pain like I would have if I'd just smashed into someone in real life, but I definitely fell. My whole avatar changed viewpoints. And I looked over to see some massive blond boy down on the floor next to me.

I heard several people laugh behind me, saying things like,

"Did you just see that?" "So embarrassing." And "They just slammed right into each other!"

Great. Six minutes in, and I'd already managed to make a complete fool of myself. Third grade all over again. So much for a new me. Old me was still coming through. And the pink hair would just make it more memorable.

Maybe I should have studied "how not to make a fool of yourself" on the internet before I came. I should have focused on things like *Don't collide into people and fall on your backside*. Or *Don't do something completely embarrassing in the first few minutes of going anywhere*. Or *Don't be Bradley Horvath*.

The program helped me halfway up, which was really disorienting.

One look at the huge blond boy, and I knew who he was—Hunter Athanasopoulos. He was the best at every sport and acted like he was already making millions and had a sponsorship with Nike. (He didn't.)

What's crazy is that, once upon a time, I thought that we might have been friends. In first grade, Hunter and I were partnered up to build a tower as high as possible in the ten minutes or so our teacher gave us. We totally rocked it. I was smart enough to build a solid foundation, and Hunter was fast and kept stacking block after block until we won. Seriously, we'd been a great team. But as soon as that was over, he was too cool for me. I was abandoned for the glittery world of popularity.

First grade can be brutal. Bubbles, building blocks, and betrayal.

And it was Hunter's friend Shawn who'd squirt-gunned me in

third grade. He's moved away, but for all I knew Hunter was the one who took the pics.

But then Hunter did something I didn't expect—he reached his hand out to help me up.

Maybe he was different now.

Wait. Oh yeah, *I* was different. There was no way he would have helped Bradley Horvath. He would probably laugh and say something like, "I'm just glad your pants are dry."

Having him help me was kind of uncomfortable, but kind of nice at the same time.

"I'm—" I almost said my real name but caught myself— "Daebak. I'm Daebak." That was the name I'd decided on. It was supposed to make me feel like I was awesome, but it wasn't exactly working.

At least he didn't know who I really was. He even started asking me questions, like he wanted to talk to me.

Maybe this was a new superpower I had, the power of amazing clothes and pink hair. Maybe I could even hang out with a guy like Hunter in this virtual school. Not that I wanted to, at least not with him. But maybe with other people that wouldn't have looked at me twice before.

He looked over my shoulder for a second.

"So what do you think about the party?" he asked.

"Well," I had to think about it. I wasn't actually prepared with an answer. What would a cooler person than me say? "It's pretty cool, I guess."

"Yeah," he said, and he looked past me again. "So what do you like to do?"

I really wasn't expecting this. Was he really just going to stay and hang out with me? "Um," I stalled. It was an easy question, but I still wasn't used to getting talked to. "I love YouTube, K-pop, and dancing, and—"

He started laughing. "Really? That's great."

"What? K-pop?" I asked. "Or did you mean—"

"Uh-huh," he said, cutting me off.

Was his tech glitching? Was his audio delayed or skipping or something? But he looked over my shoulder again.

I glanced behind me and saw two pretty girls there.

"What else?" he asked.

"Like a group I like?"

"Cool," he said, not making sense at all. Was he even listening? It clicked.

He was talking to me and pretending to listen so that he could stay close to those girls. He might even be trying to hear what they were saying. I wasn't good at the whole social thing yet, but I'd figure it out eventually. He was definitely the same Hunter Athana-thinks-he's-all-that.

But if he wasn't listening, it didn't really matter what I said. "I'm a trillionaire," I lied.

"Uh-huh," he said. Again, no sign that he'd actually heard me.

So I kept going. "And I'm vice president of the universe."

"Uh-huh," he said, tilting his head to try to overhear the girls.

Might as well go further. "I was sorry to hear about your foot fungus. I heard it's terrible. Like a forest between your toes."

He just made noises like he was listening, but he wasn't even pretending to look at me anymore.

"And I heard that some ugly aliens invaded and sucked the brains out of some people. They left their heads filled with oatmeal mush. Did they get you?"

"Uh-huh," he said.

I almost burst out laughing. Hunter had walked right into it. So hilarious. Why couldn't a video of *this* play over and over in front of the whole school for everyone to talk about?

Wait. No. Then they'd see me smash into him like a total idiot. Maybe just this part should be in front of the whole school. That would be at least a little justice.

I just wished I had someone to share the joke with, to laugh about it later. To do the whole, "Do you remember when . . ."

But I didn't.

This wasn't working. I tried. I really did. I tried to be a new me. But somehow I was still Bradley Horvath, the guy who either makes a fool of himself or you should totally ignore because he isn't worth listening to.

"Well," I said, "this conversation has been amazing, but I'm going to go." I couldn't help adding, "And don't feel too bad. Fungus is a normal part of growing up. And sorry about the mush brains."

"Yeah," he said, then started toward the girls.

I walked away alone, just like I had done so many times before.

CHAPTER 9

AUDIENCE

Edelsabeth

"Hey, Mom," I said, knowing that I was being recorded. It was kind of strange, but I'd figured out that I could take screenshots and record myself in the virtual world. I guess whoever programmed this school knew we'd want that. The program added a little phone to your avatar's hand so that everyone else would know that you were recording.

I was going to film and edit together a video to convince my mom that I'd learned all the lessons I needed already so she could send me back to in-person school.

"Here I am at the orientation party." I knew I didn't sound all that excited. I changed the camera view from selfie mode. "And I just thought you should see what the other students look like." I focused on a cute boy with black spiky hair and blue eyes. "Here's one." I switched the camera back. "And back to me." I moved the camera up to focus on a student behind me. "Here's another." I focused on a pretty dark-eyed girl in a long-sleeved mustard-colored blouse. "And there's me." One more time. A shorter girl with the cutest pixie cut, short jacket, and leggings. "Or me."

I might have been a little bitter. Everyone else looked good, like the best versions of themselves. They'd probably even made themselves a little better, like using a good filter would. Most of them weren't Hollywood level or anything, but they were all better than me.

A bunch of kids were talking, music playing in the background. I turned off my camera so I wouldn't be creepy, and decided to give this school a chance. I walked over and introduced myself to a boy named Mercelo.

"Do you like this song?" I asked, mouthing the words and bouncing a little with the beat.

"Yeah, it's a bop," Mercelo said, but turned away from me a little.

His reaction was definitely different than when I had met Jonah last year on the first day of school. Jonah was in my math class and hung on my every word, smiling, blushing. He even offered to walk up to the front and get the syllabus for me.

"Um," Mercelo added, starting to step away, "sorry, I've got to go. Nice talking to you."

"You too," I said, watching him leave, and seeing him look to the left and to the right, and then actually go back to the left.

That conversation was short. Really short. Maybe first conversations are just short like that sometimes.

Or maybe this dumb avatar was so painfully boring that I wasn't going to make a single friend here. Mom had crushed that dream to pieces, like an elephant walking on tortilla chips. If I had to look this basic, though, no one was going to know it was me.

My avatar had brown hair, brown eyes, and tan skin, but that's where the resemblance stopped. I didn't even upload pictures for this one. Doing what my mom wanted felt like I'd be showing everyone the absolute worst me every day. So I used pre-made features to build my avatar. I had cliché hair and a discount-store-looking T-shirt with a glittery star on it. My jeans weren't even fitted, and in a virtual world, for once they wouldn't be uncomfortable.

My mom said it wasn't *quite* what she had in mind, but she approved it. According to her, it would still help me realize I didn't need trendy clothes, or spending hours getting my hair and makeup just right—I didn't have to worry about trying to be pretty all the time. I could focus on the inside beauty, being the best person I could be, and focus on others. I started wondering what cheesy motivation meme she'd used to come up with all that.

It wasn't that I didn't believe it, it was just that I didn't understand why I couldn't work on both my inside and outside at the same time. And now I looked so boring, like vanilla dipped in vanilla with a little vanilla on the side. I didn't even have vanilla sprinkles.

At least no one would know it was me. I'd named my avatar Vanya, the name of my best friend back in Houston. She had been kind of my idol back in the day. Vanya could have done VR school. She was strong like that. I hoped thinking of her would help me.

If the boys from last year saw me now, I would drop so fast in the ranks. Definitely out of the top ten. Probably out of the top 100. They'd walk away, just like Mercelo had.

A loud voice interrupted my thoughts. A voice I recognized.

"Who's ready to watch a little competition?" I heard him clap a few times, trying to get those around him excited.

I knew that loud, confident, take-charge voice. I knew that clapping, that attitude.

But there was no way in the known universe that Hunter Athanasopoulos would be here. If there was anyone who would *never* come to virtual school, it was him. He was an in-person kind of guy. He loved the whole social world, hanging with friends, being the center of attention. And he was so fun to be with. Plus, athletes aren't the kind of people who choose virtual school. It's impossible to win lacrosse games with no team, no field, and no game.

But there he was; tall, a smile like he was ready to conquer the world, and that wavy blond hair that all of the girls talked about. Sure, it was a digitized version of him, but it was *definitely* him.

Absolutely.

No question.

I had no idea why he was here, but in a little flood of emotion I realized I wasn't alone. One of my friends was here with me.

And I looked terrible.

"Hey," he said, his eyes widening and a smile bursting across his face as he looked at me. Maybe it didn't matter that I looked like the plainest girl in the universe. It felt great, like all of a sudden I was back to last year where he was always quick to wink at me across the room. He lifted up his arm for a high five. "Let's do this," he said, like he was getting the crowd pumped about a lacrosse game. I guess he was talking about the basketball shooting challenge. He gave a few more high fives and got people cheering.

He didn't know it was me, right? No. He would have hugged me. At least I think he would have. But he was definitely the same old Hunter.

"I really didn't expect you here," I said, the words just coming out.

"Woooo!" he yelled and slapped hands with someone else. Most of these people had no idea who Hunter was, but he just demanded attention, and you had to react to it. Everyone was watching and smiling.

I don't think he heard what I said, probably too excited about the game that was about to start. But his eyes had definitely widened, and he smiled. That was so great to feel again.

I hadn't really told anyone that I'd be coming to virtual school. I guess I was hoping it wouldn't actually happen. But now that Hunter was here, maybe it could be better than I thought.

"So why did you go virtual?" I asked. He hadn't mentioned it either. I really wanted to know. And getting asked that by a girl he didn't think he knew wouldn't be too weird.

He didn't answer. Again. I'm sure it was bad timing or just a lot of noise. Maybe I should wait until after the game.

He clapped a few times and turned to two other girls on the opposite side of him.

I could tell what was happening the moment he saw them. He went from looking around to absolutely zoned in. Hunter said something to the girls I couldn't quite hear over the loud room and they both laughed. He had changed from talking to his audience to totally focused on them, the type of girl he'd talk to. The type he'd cross a room for.

I used to be that type.

But not here.

It hit me hard. I was in the audience. I was supposed to *watch* the cool kids, not be one of them.

I really wished I was one of those girls.

CHAPTER 10

I NEEDED A WIN

Hunter

If we were on the lacrosse field, I'd be wiping the field with this guy. It would be like a professional squaring off against my neighbor's little sister.

Or if this was *real* basketball instead of this weird virtual version, he would be epically losing. It would be like an NBA All-Star playing against a three-legged dog.

To be fair, I didn't really even know who this guy was I was playing against, but it didn't matter. I was going to win. He was voluntarily wearing a yellow tracksuit that popped out against his dark brown skin and tight black Afro. All that yellow made him look like a stylish baby duck trying to be an athlete, or a walking ear of corn.

Swish. I hit another one.

He hit one too.

Swish from me.

Another from him.

Winning isn't everything. If someone actually thinks that, they're stupid. I mean, life is still filled with awesome stuff like friends, other sports, sweet pork burritos, stand-up comedians, and movies. And the list could go on. But I do love to win. It means you squared off against others that were trying to beat you, but you beat them instead. It shows you tried harder, did better, came out on top. It builds momentum. When you try and win at one thing, it is so much easier to try the next.

And I needed a win. I needed to feel like I used to.

Months ago, I thought I was going to make the most of the last few months of school with my friends, and then barrel into the best summer ever. I had momentum. But then everything crashed.

Before I knew it, we were quarantined. It was like jail, sitting in my room staring at a computer screen for school. No friends. We texted and zoom chatted, but it wasn't anything like the real thing. There was no lacrosse—they canceled our entire season. I could go running, or play catch with my dad in the park, but that was about it. I couldn't even meet my friends at the movies, or go and get shakes. It was like the whole world was injured and grounded.

And then summer came, and it wasn't that much better. I'd been looking forward to it all year and it was a total letdown.

I didn't have to sit in boring computer classes, but our lives were canceled. And about a month in, a new problem started.

Bald spots.

Yeah. I'm almost thirteen years old, and I have two bald spots. They're both about the size of a quarter, one is just off the side of the top of my head. It happened really fast, like my hair there just decided to leave. We got on a video call with the doctor, who called it some fancy name—alopecia. I hate that word. I guess it's in my genes, but the stress could have brought it on.

I hated that too. It made it sound like I can't handle the stress, like it's a challenge I can't quite take.

The doctor said not to worry about it. I had to take some meds, and in a few months, it would probably correct itself and grow back.

That was a relief.

But then another one showed up. And what's worse is that one of them is down at the base of my skull, where I can't cover it up with a hat. I'm starting to look like a freak that got splattered with radioactive sludge or something.

But the doctor said if it got worse, if any more bald spots show up, to call him. I looked it up online, and there's a chance I could go totally bald. Like a grandpa. Like a twelve-year-old grandpa. I might even lose my eyebrows.

But the doctor said not to worry about it. And he said it like it was easy to do. Normally, I'm awesome at focusing, at zooming in on what I want, and not getting caught up in worry. But nothing else was happening. No sports. No friends. Nothing else to focus on.

The only good side to the pandemic was that no one else knew about my bald spots. I hadn't seen any of my friends. And now I didn't even have to go to regular school or anywhere else where hats weren't allowed.

That's the reason I'm here in this weird virtual school. In a few months my problem will probably go away. At virtual school, my avatar looks just like me. No one knows the difference. I'm in a place I can forget a little and be like I used to be.

So I could really use a win.

I shot again.

Swish.

But the yellow tracksuit kid was five shots ahead of me, and we were almost halfway through our time. I was losing to a guy who looked like a walking Dole Whip.

Shooting virtually took a little getting used to, but now I had figured it out, and we were both on a roll. The problem was that his roll had started before mine. I'd missed four out of my first seven, and then I went for two of the next four.

The small crowd cheered behind us. Ruby and Grace were cheering too. I really wished Kennedy and Edelle were here. When Fetu and I were on the same lacrosse team, they'd come to games sometimes and cheer. I loved knowing they were there, watching.

This wasn't lacrosse, but I'd take it.

Comeback time.

"Are you worried yet?" the yellow popsicle asked, hitting his next shot.

I was *totally* worried, but I couldn't think about that. I needed confidence. I had to turn this around. This next shot had to go in.

"Good question," I said, draining it like the league MVP under pressure. "Let me check." I hit another one. "Nope. I don't worry. I mean, I think I remember worrying once . . . when I was a baby."

In a weird way, I liked the pressure. I liked the talking. If I pretended I was going to come through, it surprised me how many times I actually did.

"You've got this," Ruby cheered.

I liked that. Despite having slammed into a kid in front of her, and though I'd just barely met her, she was cheering for me. But if I lost, that could change. There's something different about the guy who wins.

"I'm Jasper," Yellow Tracksuit said. "You're on a comeback, but if you knew me better, you'd be worried." He sank another one. And then another.

Not bad in the confidence department. I hit another two and he missed one. Both girls cheered. That filled the fuel tank a little, but I still had four to catch up and five to win. He'd probably been at this game since this party started. No. Scratch that. He'd probably found a way to get here early and practice for hours.

I shot faster, hitting three in the same time he hit two. Don't mess with the Hunter, especially when I'm on a mission to make my life awesome again.

"You're trying," Jasper said, "but it might be too little, too late."

I was still down by three.

I *really* needed a win.

"Ten," the crowd started to chant with the game, "Nine. Eight."

Time to raise things up a notch. Pretend I could do it. Focus.

I hit the next three in the time that Parker hit a pair.

Down two. More cheering.

I could do this.

"Five. Four."

Jasper recovered with another, but I hit two.

Down by one.

"Three."

Swish. Swish. Both our shots went in.

"Whoa, this is tight," Grace said.

"Two."

I moved as fast as I could. Swish.

Jasper's shot bricked. Too much pressure.

And we were tied.

"One."

With a fraction of a second left, I got another shot off, my ball arching through the air.

And then everything froze, like in the movies when time stops.

I had no idea what was going on.

CHAPTER 11

MIDAIR

Hunter

My shot was literally floating, completely frozen in time. I glanced around. Everything that wasn't a person was completely still. Darts hung in the air, bowling balls paused in their lanes—only the people could still move.

And all the music and noises from the games were gone.

"Can I have your attention?" a voice echoed through the hall. I looked around until I saw a small stage. The same woman I saw when I first logged on to the program was standing there, waving to get everyone's attention. I couldn't remember her name. Her face popped up on several ginormous screens around the room. "I can probably assume I have your attention when I pause everything else." She gave a confident smile. "Welcome, everyone, to the orientation bash. Are you having a good time?" She raised her hand to her ear, signaling for the crowd to cheer.

We did, and I was definitely louder than most people. The place was full of about as many people as had been at my school last year, probably four or five hundred of us. I think we were all excited to actually be able to interact with people again without masks. I know I was.

"Thank you," the woman said. "You've seen me before in your initial introduction. My name is Mila Holota. I'm president of NovaMillennium, the company who has made this virtual school program you'll help us test throughout this year." A little more applause. "What you experience could help us pioneer new methods in education."

She said that last statement very seriously, like this was going to make some monumental difference. Then she threw in something about a bunch of really smart people helping them design the program. "I just wanted to thank you for being here and for trying something new. That's how progress is made."

I glanced at my ball, still hanging in the air. Why had she interrupted us with all this boring stuff?

"We have a few improvements and ideas that will make school better," she continued talking. "We also have a few surprises up our sleeves, and I can't wait for you to try them."

Knowing how adults plan schoolwork, the surprises would be boring, like the party last year we earned in math when the whole class got over 80 percent on our midterm test. It turned out to be a couple bags of candy and a movie—about math. The worst. Math and parties are total opposites. They never go together.

"We'll start with the first announcement," she said. "It may not appeal to all of you, but we wanted to get some of you excited for the year. Because NovaMillennium also makes virtual reality games, we have made some available to you through the school portal, starting on the first day of school—absolutely free. These games are a little more advanced than the ones here in the rec room." Many people cheered. I didn't really know any of the games, so it didn't mean much to me, but clips popped up behind her on the screens; people in crazy armor rollerbladed down what looked like a roller coaster, people in similar armor blasted at alien spiders with light that came from their gloves, and fuzzy little puffballs ran down a colorful road with candy trees on both sides. The first two looked awesome. The last one, not so much. But it did make the crowd burst into laughter. "You can play these and other games during your break for lunch, or before or after school during approved hours," she said. "But you must maintain passing grades to do so." She paused for a moment. "After the first month of school, we will hold a tournament. You can sign up in teams of four, competing in a challenge involving any—or all—of these games. You won't know which games will be in the tournament until it begins." She smiled. "The tournament will be available for the whole school to watch, like you would for a football game or swim meet."

I could picture it. I mean, it wouldn't be as cool as actually playing lacrosse, but if people came out, it could be a big crowd. Bigger than anything else happening during the pandemic. I was definitely better at real games than virtual ones, but I had figured out this basketball thing and had been making a decent comeback.

I looked again at my ball in the air.

I might even win. I needed to win.

This tournament could be something for me to focus on, to get more momentum instead of worrying.

The lady kept talking. "And of course, whichever team wins gets automatic As and doesn't have to attend the rest of the term."

The crowd erupted, but the lady quickly calmed us down. "I am 100 percent joking with you. There's no way we could offer that." The crowd groaned, me included. "But we *will* have trophies and other bonuses." Several trophies appeared on the screen, and they actually looked really cool. Gold and silver, with action scenes from the games. "They'll be personalized to your avatars and shipped to your homes," the lady said. I wanted one. And by the sound of the crowd, a lot of other people did too.

She continued, "We'll have sign-ups after the first week of school, so get to know each other quickly and form your teams. You'll find more details posted in the school portal." She smiled one more time.

I was in. I could practice, focus, and win the whole thing.

"And now," the lady-in-charge said, "you can resume your fun."

Everything stayed frozen for a couple more seconds. The group around the basketball game turned to watch my ball hanging in midair.

The game unpaused.

My shot bumped the rim, then rolled around it.

And dropped in.

"Yes!" I pumped my fist a few times and leapt in the air.

Both Ruby and Grace cheered. Yellow Tracksuit shook his head a little, but smiled.

I could do this.

CHAPTER 12

FREE FALL

Edelsabeth

Who's the Hottest? You Pick.

I'd seen that question so many times I barely even read it.

The site did not look as professional as most sites out there, but that hadn't stopped people from logging on.

Number 1: Kennedy Alvarez.

The reigning queen.

And there she was, completely beautiful. It was natural beauty too. She wasn't wearing a ton of makeup or anything, just some basics. Her long dark hair was even back in a ponytail and she was in her volleyball uniform; tight tank top and short shorts. It was a candid shot of her warming up and laughing with other members of the team. Just a genuine smile, not taking herself too seriously.

I would know. I took the picture. And I've done videos for her. Short ones, but I do a good job catching her in action. I do decent cuts and put music to it. She has so many natural shots; she's easy to capture. And she needed new pics if she wanted to stay on top.

She was my friend. I think in some ways the list had brought us together.

I worried for Kennedy a little this year. Parker, or whoever was behind the website now, would probably make a new page for the junior high. His pages linked to our social media, and I always had to remind Kennedy to keep those updated. I could still remind her even though I wasn't at the same school, but I couldn't be there to take new pictures and send them for her to post.

I wasn't actually looking at the live site. It was a pic saved to my phone before Mom had deleted the internet browser . . .

And my Instagram . . .

And TikTok . . .

And most anything else I loved.

That was only a little bit of an exaggeration. Not only did I have to go to virtual school, but I also couldn't log on to social media. I felt totally disconnected. Amazing things could be happening, and I would have no idea. It was like I was stranded on some completely unsocial island. I could still text my friends, but I didn't know what I wanted to tell them.

Mom was definitely not my favorite person in the world anymore. Seriously, as if she wasn't already asking enough with virtual school and my avatar—and now this.

I'd given her the silent treatment since she took them away this morning.

I swiped to the next pic.

Number 2: Edelle Dahan-Miller.

And there I was.

Honestly, it was a decent pic. It had taken me about an hour to get it, and I'd chosen it over about thirty-five others; it just looked more natural. My makeup was perfect, naturally blending into my skin, and highlighting my eyelashes and brows. I have a slightly longer forehead than Kennedy, and it drives me crazy. My nose is also too round at the tip, and my eyebrows are a little too bushy, but I can pluck them until they're perfect. Mom freaked out when she caught me doing it, though.

And I looked natural sitting in my front yard on the grass, not too staged at all. I had some decent pics with my puppy, Keniv, but he wouldn't sit still long enough to get in the final one. He doesn't have the same dedication for photo shoots.

But I did get some great pictures of him. If puppies had been allowed to be rated on the site, he'd take it over.

You could submit a new pic every week on Parker's site. I just took whichever was most popular from my Insta and sent it to him.

I scrolled through more pics of me. Even in quarantine, I got some decent shots helping Mom with food, or snuggling up to watch a movie, or looking cute while catching my dad with a worried face behind me. That one's classic. Sorry again, Dad.

But none of those ideas would work now.

As part of virtual school, we could set up a personal page where we could connect to the other students. We could upload pictures or videos, post, and chat, but it was all through our avatars. It was called School MeetUp—not that cool, but I might as well make the most of it.

Because of Mom, it was the closest thing to social media I had.

I'd done the best I could, but my avatar didn't have much to offer. I got a decent angle for a candid selfie on a bench in the commons. It looked natural, not as staged as others I'd seen. But it was an avatar, so by its nature, it was staged. And where do you pose? You could stand in front of one of the games, or in the gym, but it wasn't like I could take a pic with my puppy in a blanket, or with my dad behind me.

And don't forget that my avatar was practically Ms. Boring Snoozefest. She wasn't much to work with.

I had written my short bio: *Vanya—my world is clothes, pics, chocolate, and friends. Say hi.*

Oh, and I had three friends. Not much compared to the hundreds I had on Insta and TikTok; the ones I was completely isolated from now.

But one of the three School MeetUp friends was actually Mercelo, so maybe things hadn't gone as terribly as I thought. I sent out several short messages telling people that I liked their avatars, or something fun about their bio. But no one was really posting or messaging much and I didn't want to take it more seriously than anyone else. The school was probably hoping that it would take off after the orientation party, but everyone else had real social media they could use.

Everyone but me.

"Hello, hello, hello, hello," Eva said from the hall, repeating herself over and over.

"Hey, bubs," I said.

"You looking at your phone friend?" That's what she called my phone. I told her a long time ago that I was talking to my friends on my phone and in her three-year-old mind, she meshed them together.

"Yeah," I said. If only I could take a cute pic with her and post it in the virtual school. I'd write something like *Just hanging out with the little princess*. People would eat it up.

But I couldn't here. I could take a pic in front of the mini golf, or just blur the rec room in the background, but it didn't feel the same. There wasn't much personality. I felt like I had all these talents that I just couldn't use, like a painter without a brush who was just slapping colors on a canvas.

Eva walked over and gave me what she called a tight squishy, hugging my face. It would be super uncomfortable if it wasn't so cute. And it would have been better if her cheek wasn't wet for some unknown reason. "Your phone friend is booooooring," she said. "Boring, boring. Bye." And she ran-waddled off.

She was fun, and distracting, but I wish I had my real friends.

Kennedy, Hunter, and Fetu had texted a few times tonight, and I hadn't texted back. I didn't know what to say. I guess I still kind of hope Mom won't make me go on the first day tomorrow, that she'll say I can go to regular school.

I still don't know what to do about Hunter. Part of me really wants to tell him who I am and that I'm at virtual school with him. Then I could have a friend again. Well, maybe. I just couldn't bring myself to do it. That avatar wasn't me. And she was embarrassing. If I told him, I'd have to explain all of Mom's thoughts about how I look and Parker's website and stuff. Maybe I could try to make friends with him as Vanya. Maybe that would work. But I can't tell him I'm Edelle.

I flipped back to the pic of Parker's website. When school starts tomorrow and a new site springs up, I won't be there. It will be like I did a free fall from number two into nowhere. Absolute nothing. Totally nonexistent.

I had to figure out virtual school.

I had to exist somewhere.

CHAPTER 13

BREAKOUT

Bradley

"Welcome to science class," Ms. Allen said and laughed. I wasn't really sure why she laughed; she hadn't said anything funny, and she didn't sound nervous. I guess she was just a happy kind of person. She seemed nice enough, a Black woman with long, styled hair. Maybe class wouldn't be that bad.

"Thanks," a loud voice said, "and welcome to you."

I looked across the room, and of course I saw Hunter Athana-needs-all-the-attention.

Maybe this *would* be that bad. Maybe he would start spreading the word that I'd slammed right into him during the orientation party like a complete idiot. I hadn't heard anyone mention it yet, but that didn't mean they weren't thinking it. (Or maybe because it was just first period, that wave was still coming, like a world-ending tsunami.)

Ms. Allen looked at Hunter, then laughed again. "No one has ever welcomed me to my own class before. Thank you very much." And then she turned to the whole class. "I never in a million years thought I'd be teaching virtually like this." She looked down at her own virtual collared tan shirt and jeans. "Surprise," she said, and extended her hands. This time her laugh started like a car revving up. And then it hit another gear.

I didn't really want to laugh with her. She hadn't even said anything funny, but eventually it was kind of contagious.

"Science," she said, catching her breath, "is the most interesting subject in the world."

If she was teaching the most interesting subject, it would be more like incredible ice cream flavors with daily taste-testing, or how to dance like a K-pop master in three days, or how to actually give Hunter foot fungus. I'd settle for "How to convince everyone that you're awesome when you're not."

"Seriously," Ms. Allen said, "photosynthesis is uh–*may*–zing. I mean, raise your hand if you can make your own food by just being out in the sun."

Hunter raised his hand. No surprise there.

"Yeah, right," she said, waving him off. "The only thing you make in the sun is a tan or a big red sunburn, but not food."

Hunter didn't respond. I liked Ms. Allen.

She went on to say that we'd study other things and listed a bunch, like space, plants, tides, even genetics. She said we'd learn why we are the way we are, and why some people can roll their tongue, and some people can't. I tried—I can. She said that all her students try it when she mentions it. And then—you guessed it—she laughed.

"Are you going to laugh every two minutes?" Hunter asked.

She answered, still smiling, "Probably, but . . ." In a flash her face got all sorts of serious, not even a hint of a smile or laugh left on it. "I *will* have a well-behaved class." Her head slowly swiveled, looking at all corners of the room. "And if you push me too far, I will make your life ab-so-lute-ly miserable." She ended looking right at Hunter.

He didn't move.

Then she smiled and laughed, breaking the tension. "I'm just kidding," she said, but then her face got serious again. "Kind of."

Hunter shifted in his seat.

It was official: I definitely liked Ms. Allen.

She started in on her expectations for the class, which are never interesting, even if you're a happy teacher who makes Hunter squirm. But after talking about quizzes and expectations, she said something that flipped my stomach.

"Before we go any further," she said, "you need to know each other. A good class always does. As you'll learn this semester, every good system has many parts that work together, even if they are different—*especially* if they're different. And we are going to be a *good* system." She paused, like that was something we needed to think about. "We need to feel comfortable enough to ask questions and learn together. I'm going to try the breakout room feature and give you a few minutes with a couple of your classmates. Just start to get to know them." She paused. I got the impression she was selecting buttons or something to get us started, but since it was all virtual, I couldn't really tell. "There it is," she said. "I hope this works. Have fun. Two minutes every round."

She waved goodbye to us and laughed as the room faded out.

Maybe this was good. The party hadn't gone well, but this could change things.

Or maybe this was going to be more of a total pileup than colliding with Hunter in front of everyone. I definitely didn't want to be in a breakout room with *him*. Thank goodness it was a pretty big class. I crossed my fingers.

Okay. What would pink-haired pop star me do in a situation like this?

Then I was staring at a girl I'd never seen before, an Asian girl with shoulder-length black hair.

I needed to channel my inner Daebak. It didn't matter how the party had gone. New me.

The person across from me had no idea how much of a weirdo awkward loser I was, and all I had to do was not give her any evidence of that. I opened my mouth and hoped something good would come out. "Hey," I said. Nothing too embarrassing yet.

All she said back was, "Okay." And she said it flat, with absolutely no emotion. Like, *Okay, I guess you can say hi to me.*

"My name is Daebak," I said, trying to smile.

She looked up at me. "Whatever." Still no emotion.

"So what do you like to do?" I asked.

"Not this," she said.

I began to wonder if maybe some people could see through even the coolest avatars and see the weirdo awkward loser underneath.

CHAPTER 14

UNDERCOVER

Edelsabeth

Every other girl in science class would be thrilled to be in my position right now. No, probably every other girl in this school. I've seen the way their avatars turn their heads when he comes in. Not like you could ignore him—he's a little loud.

Hunter Athanasopoulos's avatar was sitting across from me.

My nerves started acting up, but not for the reasons people might think. I still hadn't told him I was here.

He gave a big, broad smile. "Hi, I'm Hunter."

He didn't recognize my avatar from before.

Looking at him, I wanted to tell him it was me. That could change everything. I'd immediately have a friend. We might go back to hanging out at lunch, and teasing, and flirting.

But it didn't feel right. Girls who looked like me didn't hang out with Hunter. I felt like I was in gym sweats and a cucumber mask. At least I was undercover.

But maybe he'd surprise me. Maybe we could still be friends.

"I'm Vanya." It still felt weird saying my friend's name instead of mine. Immediately I remembered how friendly she was. When she would talk to you, you knew that you were important to her. We all have those voices in our heads that say awful things to us, but when I was around Vanya, those voices were just gone. I wanted to be that kind of a person.

"So, V," he said, "what do you like to do?"

Okay. Not bad. He was asking questions and even gave me a nickname. Maybe we would become friends, even if I was basic. Maybe he didn't even need to know it was me. Then I'd prove to Mom that I had learned all her lessons.

"I like clothes, taking pictures and videos, and mountain biking," I said. Then I wondered if I should have said that. There was a chance that, as he talked to me, he might figure out who I am. That was good, though, right? Then I would know that we were good enough friends that he was able to find me even in disguise. Or maybe I didn't want him to know. What if I could win his friendship even if I wasn't on a dumb website or anything?

"Dope," he said, no sign of recognition.

"What do *you* like to do?" I asked as a text buzzed my phone. That had been happening the last several minutes. I didn't check it, though. I'd have to push a button on my headset—"pass-through mode" or something. It made my view of the virtual world transparent so I could see the real world around me and check my phone. But I couldn't remember how to do it. Plus, I'd have to take off one of the gloves to use the touch screen on my phone.

The texts reminded me of regular school, the place I wished

I was. Oddly, I had one of my friends I used to text with right in front of me, not recognizing me.

"It looks like you like sports," I said, pointing at his jersey. "I'm going to guess lacrosse."

"You knew this was lacrosse?" Hunter asked, looking down. "You're awesome. Most people think it's football." And then he gave me a high five, just like at the orientation party.

"So are you pretty good?" I asked.

"I do all right," he said. "I was a starter on my club team all last year. Most of the starters are a grade above me."

"Impressive," I said.

So far, this was going better than I thought it would. But I had this feeling that made me question if we would ever actually hang out together. If you could see both of our avatars side by side, there was no way you'd think we would.

Another text came in.

"So what else?" he asked. "Like, what's your favorite food?"

Another good question. I shared, but I didn't mention things like shakshouka or falafel or any of the other foods my mom makes that might be unique enough to give me away. He was a little slow to answer. Maybe a glitch in the programming?

Another text came through, and the pause continued. Another text.

Wait. Trying not to make it too obvious, I reached up and slid my goggles off just enough to see my phone.

The texts were all from a group chat with Hunter, Fetu, and Kennedy. Hunter had started a thread.

Hunter:

> I bet you guys all wish you were
> in virtual science class.

I looked at the time stamp. He started this a few minutes ago.

Fetu:

> I love you bro, but no freaking way. 👎 👎 👎

Fetu was Hunter's best friend. They played football and lacrosse together and had a complicated handshake that ended in both of them howling. I guess the first team they'd played on together was called the Wolves.

Kennedy:

> It might be nice to just roll out of
> bed and do school in my pajamas.

And she would. I, on the other hand, got completely dressed, did my makeup and hair—I was even wearing shoes. I'd feel so uncomfortable if someone came over and I wasn't ready.

Fetu:

> It might be better than this math class tho

Hunter:

> Oh yeah. Right now, we're doing get-
> to-know-you speed chat with random
> boring people. Have to pretend I care.

I checked the time stamp. Less than a minute ago, as we'd been talking. I was "boring." It was right there on my phone. He was just pretending to care? He would never have texted that if he knew it was me—an avatar that looked like me, my name. We'd be laughing and joking.

The *only* thing different was how I looked. And my name.

We weren't on our way to becoming friends. He was just tolerating me. He was completely failing the let's-see-how-he-treats-me-when-he-doesn't-know-it's-me experiment.

Wait. Maybe I was overreacting. Maybe he didn't really mean it. But then why did he write it?

"So what else should I know about you?" he asked me. I guess he couldn't let the silence hang forever. It seemed so fake now after what he had texted.

I looked back at him in virtual school. This time I could see it. He wasn't really looking at me. Both of his hands were totally still. He probably had his gloves off and was still texting.

And I wanted to scream when I read what he texted.

Hunter:

Hey, where's Edelle? I miss that girl.

I was *right in front of him.*

CHAPTER 15

P.E.

Hunter

I needed P.E.

I needed something to focus on. Something to do. Something to help me hold things together.

I'd already taken off my glove to touch my bald spots a few times during first period. I do that almost subconsciously. It's like when you have something in your teeth, and your tongue keeps touching it. I hated it. Every touch reminds me that it's real.

I pulled out my goggles just enough to touch my eyebrows too. Just to make sure they were still there.

As long as the virtual version of P.E. was any good, I needed it. And maybe the sports in P.E. would be part of the tournament.

Maybe I could survive this.

My science teacher is a loose cannon, and I kind of like that. But the yellow tracksuit guy is in that class, and that's a problem.

You see, there are a few different types of reactions people have after they lose. There are those who respect how you won.

They realize you were cool under pressure, that you gave it your all, and you came out on top. They appreciate it. They don't like losing; no one does, but they respect your effort and heart. Now, they might work even harder because they want to beat you next time, and they might vow to never lose to you again, but you're just another warrior on a different team.

Then there are the types that, when they lose, it's like you murdered part of them, and like an action movie, they'll keep coming back to avenge their loss. You're the enemy, the villain. You're totally evil, down to your evil heart and your evil bones. And if you beat them when a bunch of people are watching, it's even worse.

If I had to guess, Tracksuit isn't exactly the respect-you type. And I definitely didn't want to be in a breakout room with him. We'd probably end up being total enemies.

I needed a distraction, so I texted my friends. It helped a lot. I still talked with everyone who showed up in the breakout room, but I also needed my buds.

Thankfully, I didn't end up in a breakout room with Tracksuit.

Since class hadn't started, and the P.E. teacher wasn't watching me, I pressed the pass-through button and read my texts.

Hunter:

Hey, where's Edelle? I miss that girl.

Kennedy, Fetu, and I had texted for a while the night before, but Edelle never joined in.

Kennedy:

I haven't seen her.

Fetu:

> Me either.

I texted her directly a few times after that, but she never responded. Had she changed her number? Wasn't attending real school? Was she mad that I hadn't told her? That would be bad, but also kind of good. At least it would mean she missed me.

It was killing me to be away from my friends. I knew it was only the first day of school, but there was a real big part of me that wanted to just ditch this whole virtual thing and show up to regular school, even if my hair was falling out. But the thought of that made me sicker than sprints in the sun on an empty stomach.

Class started with stretches. I had cleared a space in my room so I didn't bump into anything. I've been told all my life that stretching is important, but I could really use a game right now.

"NovaMillennium made us an obstacle course," our P.E. teacher explained; she was a middle-aged woman in leggings and a long-sleeved pullover. An obstacle course didn't sound bad. I'd much rather play lacrosse, but at least it was something. "If you're interested in the virtual games tournament," the teacher continued, "this might be part of that competition." All right, I could get in some practice right now. "I tried the course last week, and ended up playing for hours. And I'm not really a video game person. It's a decent workout. See what you think."

We all got up and followed her through the doors and onto a large wooden platform facing a huge room of ropes and pillars and climbing walls. If you fell, you hit the water below, like on one of those crazy game shows. It didn't look like something you'd find in a regular school. There were nets to climb, rings to swing from, moving obstacles to dodge. It would be awesome in real life, but I didn't know about it virtually.

"There are four courses," my teacher explained, and pointed at three other platforms nearby. "Pick a line and wait your turn. Once you're done, get in line for the next course. Make sure you do all four." She gave us a few instructions as to how to move and grab and dodge to overcome some of the obstacles. I thought it made sense.

"Let's do this," I said, and clapped a few times as I moved toward the front of the platform I was on. I'd let the others walk to the platforms further away. To be honest, I didn't really want to be first, but it was what a lot of people wouldn't naturally do, so I was trying to push myself. Start strong. Don't play afraid.

A few people were closer and got in line ahead of me. I was about five people back and okay with that.

As the first girl jumped off the platform, I heard someone behind me.

"Hey, man, remember me?" I turned to see a boy and a lot of yellow. Tracksuit.

Great. Not only was he in my science class, but now P.E. And since he's probably the evil type, he was back for revenge. How did I not see him? I guess I'd been so caught up thinking about Edelle and checking my texts, I hadn't really looked around.

No worries. I'd just have to focus on the course and beat him again.

Another challenge would be good for me.

Another win.

"I'm Jasper," he said, not waiting for me to answer. "We shot hoops against each other at the party."

I noticed that he said that we shot against each other, not that I beat him. *Definitely* the hate-you-and-I-want-revenge type. But I wouldn't show any nervousness. I made myself smile. "Yeah," I said, "I remember."

"A comeback win with a last-second shot?" He mimicked my shot and my celebration. "That was pretty epic. Next time don't do your clutch game-winners against me. Beat somebody else." But he said it with a smile, like he was just teasing me.

Okay, maybe I was wrong. Maybe he wasn't vengeful.

"Thanks," I said.

"Sure," he said. "Plus you were tough under pressure. I was trash-talking and everything."

I laughed.

"This looks awesome right?" he said, pointing at the course.

It did. But we only talked a few more seconds before it was my turn. Turns out Tracksuit—or Jasper—didn't actually *do* track; he liked soccer and video games. He just liked the look of the suit. He seemed much cooler than I'd thought.

"You're up," he said, nodding toward the course. Even though I was starting to think that he was the respect-you type, I still felt the pressure of him watching. He'd still want to beat me.

Time to focus.

Game on.

I launched off the pad and leapt off the top of each of the pillars. In reality, I was just running in place and jumping in my room, but the VR was actually quite convincing. I almost missed the last pillar, and thought I was going to fall, but thankfully, I pulled it off. Hopefully Jasper couldn't tell.

I had to pump my legs really fast to get all the way up the wall, and I had to move, stretch, and dodge in some intense ways to get through the course.

But I made it, and it was more of a workout than I thought it would be.

Still panting, I looked back to watch Jasper. He slid under a moving beam, then over the next. He looked pretty smooth. I didn't think he was moving as fast as I did, but he was still good. When he ended, he did a couple of those out-of-breath coughs—I was either in better shape, or he'd pushed himself a little too hard. He was really trying to show me up.

We got in the next line, and the next. We kept talking about timing ourselves to see if we could beat each other, but there wasn't really an official way. We could each count out the seconds, but there was no guarantee we would count at the right speed. And we could try to time ourselves with our cell phones, but you'd have to take your gloves off to use them, and we needed our hands to do the course.

I counted out the seconds on the next two courses anyway, and I'm pretty sure I beat him. I also tried to watch the other students when I had the chance, just to see how well they did. I thought Jasper and I were at the top.

"Hey," Jasper said, as we were waiting for the last course, "you do all right."

"Thanks, bro," I said. That felt good. I was trying hard, and I could tell all of my experience in sports helped. It wasn't perfect.

There were some things about the electronic obstacles that took some getting used to. "You too," I said. I couldn't actually see a lot of what he did since he was right behind me, but he seemed fast, and what I did see looked like he really knew what he was doing.

"You heard about the tournament they're going to have?" Jasper asked.

I nodded.

"Want to meet up after lunch and play a few of the other games?" Jasper asked. "See if we work well together?"

I noticed he didn't ask if we wanted to team up—he asked if I wanted to try them out. Maybe he was still scouting me out to see if I was good enough. Maybe he thought I was good enough to invite, but he wasn't that committed yet.

But I needed a team, and so far this guy was the best I'd seen.

It was like tryouts, and I wasn't afraid to prove myself.

"Sure," I said. "Let's do it."

CHAPTER 16

I COULD DO THIS

Bradley

Back home. Back in my domain. It had been amazing to come home for lunch at the click of a button. Do you know how many times in middle school that would have saved me? (I'm still counting.) All the pressure was off. No grabbing food then finding my corner to eat, just looking at my phone and hoping people would leave me alone, that they'd think I like being by myself all the time.

I didn't want to go back to that.

And my mom had no idea I was having a whole tube of BBQ Pringles for lunch. That was good. She'd probably take them away and make me drink/chew another mystery smoothie.

With the whole pandemic, she only went into the plumbing shop a few times a week. The rest of the time, she worked from home. I was glad she wasn't at home with me today. Dad, on the other hand, had to go in every day. Food factories can't work remotely, and they don't shut down. I do wish he'd brought me some "homemade" sweet rolls or something.

But I really didn't feel like hanging out in the kitchen and making actual food. I was thinking about doing something kind of crazy and didn't want to sit down.

We were required to go offline for thirty minutes for lunch. They said it was good for us to take time away from the goggles, plus everything had to recharge. I guess they'd thought about us all meeting in a virtual cafeteria, but then each student would have food in the real world that they couldn't see in the virtual world. And I'm sure they wouldn't want us eating around their expensive equipment. (Crumbs and VR are probably mortal enemies.)

I wiped the red BBQ dust on my pajama pants, regretted it immediately, and tried to scrape it off with my fingernail. For the record, that doesn't work. BBQ dust is basically the grape juice of potato chip flavors. Just never wipe it on anything.

After thirty minutes of lunch, the school wanted us back in the VR world, but gave us another thirty minutes of free time, time to be social, especially because of the pandemic. We could hang out in the commons, go back to the rec room, or try out the tournament games.

Before becoming a cool avatar, that had pretty much sounded like torture. Well, not the games part, but I was sure after they announced the tournament, tons of people would be there. And that was where my crazy idea was going to happen.

Something old Bradley wouldn't do. Something bold.

When they make a movie about me and my journey from

total loser to amazing greatness, this will be the beginning of the montage.

So far, the whole reinvent-me thing actually hadn't been terrible. Speed chat wasn't the absolute terror it could have been. Okay, so the first one was hard, with all those one-word emotionless answers. At the end of our two minutes, Keiko had barely given me her name. But Jordan had seemed okay. Not like we were best friends or anything, but he might talk to me again. So that was better than I usually do. And Lyla was nice enough.

I tried to talk to people in my other classes as well. I'm not sure that I'm the best at it, but I didn't feel like a total and complete failure. And when I walked through the halls, people kind of nodded to me, like saying hi. They didn't used to do that to Bradley. And on my way to English, I felt okay enough that I started walking with a little rhythm. Not like full-on dance or anything, but just a little shift-to-the-beat. And people smiled when I passed. Not like a you're-such-an-idiot smile. But more like a that's-kinda-cool smile. Or a you-do-you smile.

But I did hear a couple of whispers about me running into someone at the orientation bash. I didn't know if Hunter had been talking about it, or if they'd just seen it, but I couldn't be *that* kid again. I had to do something.

So that's where this whole idea came in. Maybe I would try something that Bradley Horvath would never do. And maybe it would even counteract that whole bump-into-someone-on-the-first-day-and-fall-down-in-the-most-public-way-possible thing. It had to. I wasn't going back to that.

I was going to dance.

I got excited and terrified even thinking about it. But it wasn't like I was going to put on a whole half-hour show or anything. I was just going to try it out. Plus, I'd practiced with my avatar. Right when the VR system boots up, before I enter the school, I can log into my avatar and change my view, kind of like looking at yourself in a security camera when you walk into a store. So I can dance and watch it. And thankfully, it actually looks pretty impressive. At least, I think so, and I've watched a lot of dance videos. It wasn't round Bradley doing the moves—it was smooth Daebak.

You know in those YouTube videos when you see someone who can dance on a busy sidewalk or something? Sure, it's a little awkward at first, but then gradually people stop and watch, and then more and more people watch, and soon there's a decent little crowd there. Maybe a few of them even film it. I was going to do that in the hallway from the commons to the games, at least for a few seconds. I mean, I was trying to talk myself into it.

But maybe not. Maybe I should practice some more. Or just rest up and watch some music videos and scroll through TikTok. I could try my crazy idea tomorrow or something.

I'm not sure I even had to go back for social time. I doubt they kept track of that. What were they going to do? Discipline me for missing recess? That didn't sound like a thing they'd do.

But maybe it wouldn't be terrible. I'd always wanted to try, and maybe it would go okay. Or maybe it would go amazing, and I would get a crowd. That would be seriously pow.

Daebak was different from corner-sitting, phone-staring Bradley, right?

I sat there eating chips, thinking in circles, breaking out into practice dance moves until lunchtime was over. Others were probably going into the program to play and talk.

I'd go back after this chip. I crunched down on it, feeling the BBQ dust giving me bravery. But not enough.

One more. Crunch.

Or a couple more. Crunch. Crunch.

Or maybe . . . I should wait.

But that was such a Bradley decision. I didn't want to stay the same as I'd always been. But I would if I just did everything that I usually did. I wanted friends. I wanted to be able to be me somewhere outside of this apartment.

And Daebak was already doing better than Bradley—he wouldn't hide in his living room.

At least not much longer.

I took a deep breath and looked at my VR equipment.

I could do this.

After one more chip. Crunch. And maybe . . .

Nah. I set down the chips, brushed off my fingers, and put on the goggles.

And then I tapped the pass-through button so I could see well enough to eat one more chip. Just in case I needed it.

Then I clicked in.

CHAPTER 17

SENT

Edelsabeth

Lifting my goggles, I looked at my text again. Should I send it?

Edelle:

> Hey, sorry I didn't tell you before, but I'm actually going to that virtual school this year. My mom's making me.

It's not like I could keep it a secret forever.

But I wondered how Hunter would react. He'd ask where I was, but did I want him to find me? Maybe he'd remember what I said about designing clothes, taking pictures and making videos, and mountain biking, and it would click. He'd realize it was me and apologize. The way I looked wouldn't matter, and then we'd be friends in this crazy school together.

Or maybe he wouldn't figure it out.

But I wasn't going to tell him it was me. At least not yet. Because then if he didn't want to be friends, or if he acted like he wanted to be friends at first and then just gradually started paying more attention to other people and left me behind, that would be impossibly awkward. I'm not sure my heart could take it. And not only would I be embarrassed to look the way I do, but completely mortified that we weren't really friends at all.

If he didn't figure it out, maybe I could make friends with him again, even though my avatar was boring and basic. Maybe that would even prove to Mom that I don't need to be pretty all the time.

My avatar was walking slowly through the virtual school as I kept glancing down at the phone in my real hand, debating whether to send the text. I moved through the commons toward the games. I had considered trying them out, but shooting monsters in imaginary worlds wasn't really my style. Maybe if we just stopped shooting them, the monsters would be nice.

I read my text one more time, took a deep breath, and pushed *send*.

"Whoa," a voice said.

I looked up to see another avatar dodge out of my way.

"I'm so sorry," I said. "I was trying to send a quick text, and I just wasn't—"

"It's okay," he said and smiled.

"Wait," I said, my mind realizing what had been happening, "were you . . . dancing?" It seemed like it. Like as I was walking by, he went from standing to breaking into a move. I just hadn't expected it. I felt bad that I'd thrown him off.

"Yeah, kind of," he said, and looked to the side, like he was a shy rock star. I had seen him in my science class. I'd admired his hair and how it faded beautifully from dark brown into pink. I guess computers can do that. He was also wearing a super unique magazine-cover-worthy jacket with jeans. I loved all of it.

I immediately wished my avatar looked like me. Call my mom, cancel this, and just make me look like me.

But I couldn't do that.

"Again, I'm so sorry," I said.

He gave a crooked smile. "No worries. I actually crashed into someone else the other day," he said. Then he shook his head. "I don't know why I told you that."

I couldn't picture that happening to him. He seemed like he'd have great body control. I laughed. "I guess we all mess up a little," I said. That's when I could have just moved on, but I didn't want to. "I'm . . . Vanya," I said.

"Nice," he said, smiling, then added. "I mean, nice to meet you." He was probably too cool for me and politely going through the motions. Or maybe he was going to leave in just a second like Marcelo had. Or pretend to listen to me but start texting someone else to say that I was boring.

But he said it was nice to meet me. I had to try to keep this going. "You too," I said. "That's really pink." I pointed at his hair. It was a dumb thing to say but I was a little nervous, and it just popped out.

"Yeah," he said, then looked away, like he was movie-star smooth, staring out into the distance. Or like he wanted to go somewhere else. I felt like I was falling into the audience again, disappearing into the background.

"I was nervous to go pink at first," he said. "I mean, it's pretty bold. But then . . ." he paused for a moment, "I just did it. I regretted it for a little bit, but not now."

"It looks great," I said. "Really pops." It made me wonder if I would be brave enough to try something so different. I usually chose styles that I had already seen others succeed with on social media, like makeup to bring out my eyes or clothes that complement my body type—not something to stand out as different, like pink hair or neon boots. I could feel my admiration rising for this kid.

I hated the idea he might not give me a chance to be friends just because I had a basic avatar. It doesn't really make sense that we end up grouped together according to how we look, and then we only make friends in that group.

I could overcome that, right? I could become his friend? I've seen people on social media who aren't classically beautiful become really popular. What did they do? I didn't know, but I had to say something before he left.

"Show me your dance," I said, hoping he wasn't about to walk away.

He smiled. "I was just . . ." He hesitated and gave a nervous smile.

"I'm sure it's awesome," I said.

He bit his lip a little and nodded. Not only was he not leaving, but I thought he might actually show me. He shifted to the left, his arms moving to one side, then his legs spun him back. He was pretty good. "It's the dance to an Avalanche song," he explained.

He quietly sang a couple lines while he moved some more,

and I instantly recognized it and joined in just a little, nodding and singing along as I remembered the words. I definitely didn't dance.

It was adorable how he sang quietly, like he didn't have an amazing voice. And as I sang, his moves got even better, sharper and right on the rhythm. He was probably just months away from breaking through into the big time and making records.

"I've got an idea," I said. "I like to make videos. Can I record this?" I needed something more interesting and better to post than just me on School MeetUp. And he was definitely interesting and super talented. Of course I'd get his permission before posting, but first I needed to record it.

He smiled pretty big. "Sure, I guess."

And then he moved a little more. I could tell he was nervous and trying not to look at other people too much as they walked by, but now that he was warmed up, his moves were stone-cold professional good. And I could shift the camera angles to make it look a little more like a music video than just a regular post-on-your-feed recording.

It only lasted thirty seconds or so, but I could tell he liked it. I was like his personal videographer, producing something awesome for him. And I think it changed the feeling of the whole thing. He wasn't just randomly dancing in the hall; people walking by could see creation in action.

I was making him feel cool.

A couple people even cheered a little for him as they walked by.

"I'll send this to you," I said when he was done. "If you're okay with that." He definitely was. And then I found out his name was Daebak. How cool was that? I had to remember it. It was like the word *day* and then Bach, that famous composer guy. We talked about a few more things, like we found out we both liked superhero movies. Well, at least the fun ones. Not the type that get all dark and broody or crazy violent. And he laughed and smiled a little more.

Maybe he wasn't too cool for me. Maybe I could make friends with an about-to-be-a-rock-star kid even with a super vanilla avatar.

My phone buzzed in my pocket; I realized I'd received several texts over the last few minutes. But I wasn't going to check them now. Hanging out with Daebak was so much better than I thought this free time would be.

"Hey," a voice said, "I know you."

At first, I thought someone was talking to Daebak, but I turned to see Hunter Athanasopoulos, his smile as big as ever. And he was talking to me.

He found me.

CHAPTER 18

I KNOW HER

Bradley

I definitely wasn't dancing in front of a million screaming fans, but it kind of felt like it.

No huge crowd formed. There were a couple of cheers, but not really any clapping. Still this was amazing, awesome, seriously pow, totally daebak.

I *was* Daebak.

It was the first time anyone other than my parents had seen me dance—and I kind of love it.

Vanya actually wanted to record it. My mind was blowing up over and over again, like fireworks at the end of a huge concert. Like the grand finale, booms and sparkles lighting up the sky bigger than lightning.

No one has ever wanted to record me. Well, not for anything good, anyway.

She even seemed to know what she was doing, getting interesting angles as I moved. Plus, she would have to friend me on MeetUp in order to send it. That would mean we could talk again.

I almost couldn't believe my crazy dance-in-public idea had actually worked.

Unless somehow the whole thing was to make fun of me. Like, I'd get the video and look all stupid, and then people would be sharing it through the whole school again. And instead of pee-his-pants kid, or the weirdo-who-walked-right-into-Hunter kid, I'd be the-kid-who-thought-he-could-dance-but-couldn't. And then Vanya would be a terrible villain, a double agent in the movie sent to destroy me.

No. I didn't think that was right. Vanya wouldn't do that; it was like she was a crowd of fans all in one person. Or at least that's how I felt. Or maybe I was overreacting because that had never happened before.

But then Hunter Athana-spoil-everything-all-the-time had to come along.

And, of course, he knew Vanya.

"You're in my science class, right?" he asked her.

"Yeah," she said.

"Vanessa?" he guessed, then shook his head. "No. It's some-thing like that, but not."

"Vanya," I corrected. I guess he didn't know her too well.

"Right," he said and clapped. "That's it. I remember the glit-ter star shirt." He pointed down at her shirt. He turned to me. "And Pink Hair," he said. He didn't try to say my name. I doubt he remembered it at all. Hopefully he wasn't about to tell Vanya about me knocking him over at the orientation party.

"I'd love to hang and stuff, but right now I'm looking for my friend," he said. "She's about your height, V." He pointed at Vanya. "Really cute. Long dark hair. Tan skin. Her name is Edelle. Have either of you seen her?"

There was something about the way Vanya shook her head that I totally understood. I had felt that way over and over again. That strange mix of I-wish-you-remembered-me-better and I-was-kind-of-hoping-you-were-coming-to-talk-to-me. Hope rising up a little, then hope crashing down, an emotional jump from the roof.

Hunter looked at me, waiting for an answer.

"At this school? No," I said and shook my head. I remembered Edelle. We'd had a couple of classes together last year. In fact, just hearing her name probably made me have the same look Vanya had. At the beginning of last year she'd been new, and she talked to me a little before Mr. Richardson's class. (She was also in keyboarding class with me, but sat in a different row. We didn't really talk then, but she waved a few times.) She might have only talked to me because she was new, but I still liked it. Not a lot of people did that. But then things changed. She started getting more attention and more friends, and she didn't talk to me anymore. And one day, I was walking by her table at lunch, and I overheard someone telling her about the whole pee-on-stage incident and then everyone laughed. Sure, the others were louder, but she giggled right along with them. It was like I was the funniest meme of the year.

I also saw her do something in keyboarding I didn't like. I

couldn't know for sure, but she might have done something really mean to Marie Holland.

"Okay," Hunter said, "if you bump into her, tell her I'm looking for her." And then he gave a big Hunter Athana-my-life-is-perfect smile. "See you in," he paused to remember, "science." And then he looked at me. "And make sure you watch where you walk."

There it was. My heart dove off the roof as he walked farther into the commons.

I glanced over at Vanya, but she didn't look back. She didn't seem like she was going to ask about what Hunter just said. She was still watching him. He stopped to talk to Keiko, the girl in science with the one-word answers. She was just standing there by herself. Hunter was probably asking if she had seen Edelle too. She hardly gave him a reaction. That girl's a vibe. At least she's consistent. But she also watched him leave.

Vanya was still watching him too.

Hunter had that effect on people, especially girls. I didn't get it. At all. And I didn't like it.

"I know her a little," I said, trying to break Vanya out of her trance.

"Who, her?" Vanya asked, pointing at Keiko.

"Well, yeah," I said, "that's Keiko, but I meant Edelle."

Her eyebrows wrinkled for a second. "Really?" she asked.

I nodded. Maybe I was reading too much into this, but I didn't like how Vanya seemed to wish she was her, or thought that she was being overshadowed by her.

"She's okay," I said, "but you're a lot better."

I believed it. I'd only known Vanya for a few minutes, but she'd already done more for me than Edelle ever had. She treated me like I was a rock star. And she hadn't ignored me *or* laughed at me.

Well, I guess that was assuming this wasn't all a terrible joke or that Vanya wasn't a double agent. Or that she wasn't going to start ignoring me when she got more friends.

I didn't think she would. Vanya didn't seem to be the type to get all caught up in popularity and looking good in front of people. She seemed awesome.

But I really couldn't understand the look she gave me when I said it.

CHAPTER 19

GIANT ALIEN SPIDERS

Hunter

A giant alien spider scurried down the hall at me with impressive speed, its spiny legs gripping and ripping into the floor as it moved. It was the size of a large dog, with a sleek red shell and slime dripping out of almost every part of it.

"Die, you evil nasty goopy thing!" I yelled, aiming my glowing gloved hand at it. I tried to adjust for the monster's speed as I punched forward and a ball of light rocketed from my fist. But the spider was crazy fast. I punched out balls of light again and again, managing to injure two of its legs, and hitting it once in the body. But it just wasn't stopping.

"Evil nasty goopy thing?" a voice sounded in my ear. "Is that a technical term?" It was Jasper, the kid in the yellow tracksuit. He was shooting at my spider's sister, or brother, or weird uncle. "I mean, it's accurate," Jasper said. "It's just a mouthful."

"Yeah," I said, and calculated one more time before shooting, "maybe let's just call them goopies for short." I punched again, nailing it right between the eyes.

Okay, I admit that's not as impressive as it sounds. These things have like seventeen eyes so there's a broad target, but my shot definitely hit between at least two of them. Maybe between like six of them. Instead of squirting blood or dissolving into purple slop or something, it just burst into mist and blew away. I guess that's how the goopies die.

Now I only had to worry about nine of his cousins that were still in the hallway. Not to mention any others that might show up.

I still couldn't find Edelle, and she wouldn't respond to me. I didn't get that. Maybe she was just busy? But why would she send the text, and not think I'd want to see her? I spent so much time looking for her that I was late to meet Jasper, and then we only had ten minutes until class. I'd texted her that I was trying to find her everywhere but couldn't, and that I'd be here shooting alien spiders. For all I knew she could be watching me right now.

"Can we tell if anyone is watching us play?" I asked.

"I think the program has an option to see the crowd if there's anyone there," Jasper said, "but I doubt there is. Anyone else could just jump in and play if they wanted to."

The program wasn't showing me any options to see anyone watching. She probably wasn't there.

Edelle had said that her mom was making her go to virtual school. But that didn't make a lot of sense. Why would her mom do that? Then again, my friends wouldn't have any idea why I was here either.

Was there a chance that when Edelle found out that I was

coming here, she'd enrolled? That would be so dope. So much effort and a really good friend. And it would be great to have her here, especially while I was trying to not worry about my stupid bald spots. Even just thinking about hanging out with her felt good. I'd love to see her.

But for now, breaking into a monster's lair, defeating its army of alien spider goopies to save the world was a good distraction.

"Take that, goopy!" Jasper yelled, shooting another spider with his fist guns and watching it vanish away. "Hey, that does kind of help."

He shot with almost each word, almost every ball of light finding its mark. Two more goopies misted. The kid was good.

"I think I've shot seventeen," Jasper said. "How about you?"

"Fifteen," I admitted. Of course he knew he was ahead.

"So, just for clarification," Jasper said, "who's shot more?" He coughed to clear his throat.

"Less talking. More shooting," I said.

Like in most video games, I'd expected to get a different avatar, the super-soldier kind who looked like he could bench press five hundred pounds while shooting a blueberry off a goalpost sixty yards away. I don't know why a blueberry would be on a goalpost. That doesn't make sense. But you get what I mean.

But both Jasper and I looked like our student avatars inside the video game, me in my lacrosse jersey and him in his yellow tracksuit. The game had given us cool armor over our arms and legs, a sort of helmet, and the amazing light-shooting gloves, but you could still see glimpses of our clothes, which, with those colors, couldn't be good for camouflage. If I were an alien spider, I'd want to eat Jasper just so I didn't have to look at that tracksuit anymore. Or because I'd mistaken him for a very large mango.

But it did make the game feel more real.

"Don't get too cocky," Jasper said, spinning around. "This game is called *Infestation ExtermiNation* for a reason." Jasper was starting to sound like a coach. I wasn't sure I liked that.

"Me, cocky?" I asked. "Who's the guy counting kills?" I jogged farther down the abandoned shopping mall hallway. In the game, this was where the nasty goopies had landed. We were searching for their den, where the mother of all these ugly terrors was hiding out. I held out my fists, ready for anything.

I hoped Jasper thought I was good enough. Together we'd have a decent shot at the tournament.

A goopy burst out, and we both shot it twice at the same time, exploding it into mist.

"Jinx," Jasper said.

"I don't think you can call jinx killing aliens," I said. "That's only when you say the same thing at the same time."

Jasper just smiled. "You owe me a soda."

"Whatever," I said, raising my glowing fists again. "Sixteen."

"Fifteen and a half," Jasper corrected. "Come on, Lacrosse. I'm at seventeen and a half. Keep up." Then he bolted down the hall. "I need to get ready for that trophy."

He said *I* and not *we*.

I shot another alien that burst through the wall to the side, a new one this time, some kind of alien scorpion with long pincers. I had to roll away as it reached for me, then twisted back to shoot it.

"Epic!" Jasper yelled.

We shot and moved our way through the next few rooms. Being honest, Jasper was better. The more we went through, the more I wondered what he thought of me. So I took it up a notch as we went on, slipping into rooms first to take out a few alien beetles. Apparently there were more of those than spiders, and they counted for more points. I even got off the first shots at a massive Martian centipede. Then it nearly ran me over, but we eventually destroyed it.

What I didn't have in video game experience, I was learning to make up with in body control.

Then I got a text, and pushed pass-through on my goggles to check my phone really quick in case it was Edelle.

Nope. It was Fetu asking if I had found her yet.

Then an alien spider ate me.

I hoped Edelle wasn't watching.

CHAPTER 20

RUN

Hunter

"You getting soft?" my older brother Ryker asked and then ran a little faster.

"Whatever," I said, catching up to him. "You're not even challenging me, old man." He's only eight years older, but that was still old.

"Oh, yeah?" he asked, way more sweat pouring down his face than mine. Well, I couldn't really see my own face, but there was no way I was sweating that much.

"Yeah," I said. I used to really struggle to run as far as he did and keep up. But now, I was hanging right with him, even after his Navy training and everything. He was home on leave for the month.

He kicked it up a notch, and so did I.

It felt good. The burning in my legs meant I was doing something, accomplishing something. We were on an early-morning run before school. Hopefully it would help me focus and get rid of some worry. And to keep me from thinking about Edelle. She still hadn't responded. I didn't get that. Did she not like me anymore? There wasn't any way she knew about my bald spots, right? I checked my baseball cap that I had on backward. If someone really knew what they were looking for, they'd see the spot on the back of my neck.

"You're still in charge of your life," Ryker said, his legs pounding, sweat running down his buzzed head.

"What?"

"All of this," he said. "Your new school. Your attitude. Even your problem," he looked up at my hat. "*You're* in charge. *You* decide how to act. *You're* the captain of this journey."

"No, I'm not," I said.

"Yes—you are," he said. This was his military training coming out. "That's one of the secrets to success. *You* are always in charge of *your* life." I'd heard coaches say it too. *You've got to believe the fate of the game is in your hands. You can do this.*

"Most of the time," I said, "but not always." I mean, school definitely wasn't in my control. I couldn't control everyone there. Or why Edelle wasn't telling me where she was for some reason.

"No excuses," he said between deep breaths.

"What if I was kidnapped by terrorists, blindfolded, and forced to yodel for like twenty-seven hours straight? Then I wouldn't be in charge of my own life."

My brother took a minute to answer that, running hard while he thought. "First off," he said, still keeping a good pace, "those would be really strange terrorists. The yodeling would hurt them more than you."

"You know what I mean," I said.

"Yeah," Ryker said, "maybe I should say that no matter what happens, you're in charge of *you*. With the terrorists, you might not be able to choose everything." He panted, and took a few more steps. "But you could choose to not break in front of them, that you won't show fear. You could choose to not give up on the hope that it still could turn out okay."

He wasn't convincing me. "Imagine that *you* woke up with your hair falling out at twelve, you spend all day inside going to a weird school full of weird people, one of your friends seems to be purposefully ditching you, and you don't know why. I don't get to choose that."

"Your school is definitely unusual," he said, "but you chose it. You had your reasons, but now you have to make the most of it. And you can't control your hair, or other people, but you can still choose to do your best. To hope for the best. To reach out to try to find your friend." He panted more as he ran. "But no matter what happens, you choose your attitude and make your own decisions."

I was trying to hope for the best about my hair, but it was hard. I worried all the time. I'd woken up last night and couldn't go back to sleep because I just kept thinking about it. What if it gets worse? What if I lose my eyebrows? What if I went totally bald? When I finally fell back asleep I dreamed I'd lost all of my hair and everyone laughed at me, especially Edelle. She thought I was a complete freak. My other friends didn't want to hang out. No girls were interested.

I checked my hat again.

"I'm in charge," I whispered to myself, under my breath.

CHAPTER 21

UNBELIEVABLE

Bradley

Something unbelievable happened.

It wasn't like everyone clapped for me as I came into science class, and then K-pop started playing, so I started dancing, then half the class got up and danced exactly with me, like an entourage completely in sync—but I was still clearly the focus of the whole number. And then the song built, and the lights started flashing, and then glitter exploded from the ceiling, and I did a backflip and landed in the coolest of cool poses right when the music ended, and hundreds of dollar bills slowly drifted to the ground.

That would be unbelievable.

But it didn't happen.

Something else unbelievable did.

I stepped into science class and the desks were pushed together in groups of four to make tables. (That's not the unbelievable part yet. And I guess *pushed* wasn't the right word because they were virtual. Maybe Ms. Allen could just choose a setting and it would just arrange them that way.)

But Vanya was sitting at a table talking to Hunter. (The unbelievable's still coming. Wait for it.)

She was talking to him kind of like they were friends, like he wasn't a cocky athlete who stomped on everything awesome. And, of course, she really seemed like she wanted to talk to him. I couldn't compete with a guy like that. I mean, I could compete in all the important stuff like having a heart and not being stuck up. But he made me so uncomfortable, and sometimes he made me as angry as watching the rich mother-in-law in movies whose daughter is dating a poor kid. (Seriously—those ladies are meaner than boars with porcupine quills between their toes.)

But Vanya was worlds cooler than Hunter. She'd sent me the video she made, and I think my jaw is still on the floor. She added the Avalanche song to the background, put it through a few filters, and made some fun cuts where I'd repeat a move to the beat. It was pretty short, but she made me look highlight-reel professional. And then she asked if she could post it.

I definitely gave my permission.

Someone actually filmed me and wanted to post it for a reason other than to make fun of me. And she wrote, *This is Daebak, and he's got style. I mean, check out that hair and the drip. And the moves!*

No one had ever done anything like that for me before.

I think I reread that post and rewatched the video like every fifteen minutes.

And people liked it. I had twenty-three people request to

follow me. And that was just since yesterday. That was more social-media friends than I've ever had.

So that was unbelievable, but then something else unbelievable happened on top of it. Vanya saw me and waved me over to sit with her.

Yep, she had Hunter right there, and she quit looking at him to invite me over.

No one ever invited me over.

Daebak was *definitely* different from Bradley.

On my way, I saw Keiko. "Hi, Keiko," I said.

"Why?" she said.

I still didn't know how to respond to her. Yesterday after school I'd said hi as well and asked how her day was. She said, "It's like treading water in a deep sea of social meaninglessness." I didn't know how to respond to that either.

So I went and sat next to Vanya.

A girl invited me and I went over, even with Hunter there. I almost felt like I could compete with him. Like maybe someone might pay attention to me, even if he was there.

"Hey, Pink Hair," Hunter said as I sat down.

"His name is Daebak," Vanya said. Not only did she make amazing videos, but she remembered my name. And she corrected Hunter about it, just like I'd corrected him about Vanya's name yesterday.

Hunter didn't really respond to her correction. "Did you find Edelle?" he asked.

I shook my head.

"Neither of you did, huh?"

"Daebak knows her," Vanya said.

"What?" I said. It took me by surprise. I didn't want to talk about Edelle with Hunter. I'd rather talk with Vanya. "We had a couple of classes together last year," I explained, hoping we'd move on.

"Balderstein Middle?" Hunter asked. "I'm not surprised. Everyone there knows her. She's top five." He turned to Vanya, "There was this website of the most popular girls and she was always right there at the top." He put his hand above his head to symbolize the top.

It bugged me the way he said that. "No," I said, "it's this dumb site where boys rate how hot they think the girls in school are." I had looked at it a couple of times because so many people were talking about it. And it *was* stupid; it didn't even look good. And if they did a site like that for boys, I would have been the reigning champion of the bottom, the king loser of the basement of nobodies. ("Welcome to the bottom floor, please enjoy your stay in the furthest-from-luxury, definitely-not-a suite of the lonely and invisible.")

"Yeah, okay," Hunter said, and then gave me a look. I might have ticked him off a little, but right then, I was okay with that. Bradley would have tried to stay under the radar, but Daebak didn't really have a reason to.

Hunter pointed at me. "I don't remember the pink hair."

"What?" I asked. "Yeah, you do. You literally call me Pink Hair. You don't even know my—"

"No," he interrupted. "Like at Balderstein Middle. I don't remember anyone with pink hair," he said.

Oh, no. What had I done? He didn't recognize me because Daebak didn't go to Balderstein Middle. There wasn't anyone there with bright pink hair. But he definitely knew Bradley. Was there any way Hunter could figure out that Daebak was really Bradley Horvath? My mind raced, trying to think about what Hunter knew about me here. We'd smashed into each other the first day, and then he ignored me while he was trying to talk to some girls. But he knew I got distracted sometimes. That was definitely a clue. And now he knew I went to Balderstein Middle last year. He knew I knew Edelle. So far, I was probably safe, but this whole thing made me uncomfortable.

"The pink hair's new this year," I said, trying to cover up. That was true, but I hoped it was enough to throw him off the trail.

Hunter looked me up and down for a second, then shrugged. "If you like it," he said.

"I like it," Vanya said.

"Thanks," I said. If I had almost completely blown my cover, at least Vanya was there to give me a compliment.

But Hunter wasn't really listening anymore. He saw a friend in yellow warm-ups walk in. Hunter waved him over.

I hoped I hadn't just ruined everything. Things were going way too well to have old me ruin the new one.

CHAPTER 22

LIKE ME

Edelsabeth

I had been thinking about it ever since Daebak said he knew me at lunch. While I edited his dance video I kept looking at his face, trying to remember anyone who looked anything like him.

The more I looked at him, the more confused I was.

He'd said he knew me from school. But that didn't make sense. I went through my entire yearbook three times last night. There were no Daebaks. The closest *D* names were two Davids and a Darrell, but they didn't look like him at all. In fact, no one did. No pink hair. No rock star look.

And I didn't remember anyone dancing in the hallways at Balderstein Middle. I mean, I guess there were some theater kids who did that a little, but it was a different kind of dancing.

He knew about the website, so that was definite evidence he'd gone to school with me last year. So he wasn't lying. But he didn't like the site—that was definitely different. Most guys seemed to be all over it.

"Thanks for that video," Daebak said, after a pause. He was kind of frozen there for a second. He leaned forward as he spoke. I think he wanted to talk without including Hunter and his friend. "You did an awesome job."

"You're welcome," I said. "If you want, let's do another one."

His eyes got huge. "Definitely."

I really had fun putting it together; I hadn't edited a video like that for a while. Of course, most of my videos had been either my own or for Kennedy, so this felt different. Plus, with the pandemic going on, it was nice to have a creative project. Mom was all worried at first; she thought I was obsessing about my profile, or had found a way back onto social media. She almost went all mama bear. But when I showed her that I was doing it for someone else at school, she seemed surprisingly okay with it.

And it had the most views on my profile so far. It wasn't anything like my views on Insta or TikTok, but maybe it could help. Plus, it seemed to make Daebak really happy. And so far, I liked hanging out with him.

But I couldn't figure out why he said what he did. He liked virtual me more than Balderstein Middle me.

"Sorry he keeps bugging you about her," Daebak said, nodding over at Hunter.

"What?" I said.

"Edelle," Daebak explained. "I think he's pretty obsessed. I saw them together a lot." I glanced over at Hunter, who was shadowboxing while talking to an avatar in a yellow tracksuit about a game. It was amazing how fast he came looking for me after I sent the text. And at first I thought he'd actually found me in just minutes, like he put together the clues and knew that I was Edelle and wanted to hang out.

That would have been impressive.

But it hadn't happened.

He'd been texting me nonstop, asking where I was and if we could meet up. Part of me really wanted to, but the other part of me knew he wasn't interested in Vanya, only Edelle. And I wanted to know why. And I had to prove to Mom that I didn't need to focus on my looks. That if I was an amazing person inside, I could still live and make friends and be successful. One of the best ways would be to make friends with Hunter again.

The only response I texted Hunter was, "Let's see if you can find me."

But right now, I was right in front of him.

BRRRRRIIIINGGG

"Take your seats," Ms. Allen said. She stood at the front of the room, not laughing and not smiling. "Hunter, Jasper." She looked at the two friends on the other side of the table and waited for them to quiet down. I guess Jasper was the boy in the tracksuit.

"Good morning again," Ms. Allen said and laughed. Now that everything was in order, apparently she was happy. "Today I want you to work in groups." And another laugh came out. "Well, it's more like a game. We'll have you work together with the people seated at your table." She circled her fingers in the direction of each table to help us get the idea. It would be me, Daebak, Hunter, and his friend.

This was good. I could hang out with Daebak, and maybe I would remember how I knew him.

And maybe working together with Hunter would help me become friends with him again, even if I was Miss Vanilla Boring-pants. Or maybe he would figure out it was me and show that looks don't really matter.

I looked at Hunter and then at Daebak. One had to figure out who I was, the other I had to figure out who he was.

A huge realization hit me. Hunter couldn't find me yet because I didn't *look* like me. Maybe I couldn't find Daebak in my yearbook because he didn't look like anyone in my yearbook.

Maybe he was undercover just like me.

CHAPTER 23

LIKE A SLUG VILLAIN IN A SPACE MOVIE

Hunter

Ms. Science Teacher said my favorite word any teacher can say in class: *game.* Maybe she was all right. I just hoped it was a decent game, and not one of those stupid activities that teachers call a game. Like a worksheet *game.* Or a let's-time-you-while-you-do-a-worksheet *game.*

But it was a group thing, and apparently I was stuck with Pink Hair. V was all right. At least I had Jasper.

Wouldn't it be amazing if Teacher Lady sent us into *Infestation ExtermiNation* and we all shot alien bugs? I don't know what that would have to do with science class, but I would love it. I mean, it's science fiction, so there is that. Jasper and I would tear it up. Pink Hair would probably get distracted and walk into some aliens. And I didn't know V very well, but I couldn't imagine that she was the type to love virtual games.

"Okay," Ms. Science Teacher said, "you have just a minute to make sure that you know everyone in your group and decide on a team name. And then I'm going to see what you already know about some of the science we'll study this year."

I don't know why she always wanted us to get to know each other. I guess that was her thing. Well, that and laughing all the time.

"I don't know Jasper," V said.

"He's awesome at *Infestation*," I said, and reached out for a high five.

"Thanks." Jasper high-fived me back.

This was a perfect chance for him to say that he and I were going to enter the contest together, but he didn't.

Whatever.

I would practice and practice, and even if I didn't team up with him, I'd find somebody else. And we'd win.

Jasper met the other two and high-fived them both. When they said their names I tried to remember them. I didn't want either of them correcting me about that again. But I still couldn't remember Daebak from Balderstein Middle.

"What should our team name be?" Vanya asked.

"Maybe the Archers," I said. "That's my favorite lacrosse team."

"Not all of us are into that, though," Jasper said.

"Or, like, Avalanche," Daebak said.

"Not bad," Jasper said.

It sounded pretty cool, like the hockey team in Colorado.

"We could take the first two letters of everyone's name," Vanya said, "and make a word out of it, like Ja-Va-Hu-Da." She said the name slow, thinking about it as she went.

Jasper laughed. "That's it. It sounds totally crazy."

"I'm okay with it," Pink Hair said.

And that was it. We got a stupid name that fast. We were JaVaHuDa. It wouldn't exactly intimidate anyone and it sounded like the giant slug villain in a space movie. Vanya entered our team name somewhere.

"Time's up, " Science Teacher said. "Now you're best friends. Enter in your team names if you haven't already." She surveyed the room for a second. "I'm trying to stretch myself and try out the programs the virtual school makes available to us. I hope this works. If it does, you will compete as a team, helping each other out. Each team plays against the other teams in the class. The faster you get the right answer, the more points you get. But of course, getting the *right* answer slower is much better than getting a *wrong* answer quickly." She paused and moved her arms. She was probably starting the program. "If the program doesn't work, we can do a worksheet."

Everyone groaned.

"Let's hope it works, then," she said. "Whichever team gets the highest average gets a two-percent boost on the next test."

I waited for her to take the prize away, like Head Lady over the Virtual Program had done.

"I'm serious," she said. "It could bump you from a B+ to an A-."

It wasn't the highest of stakes, but I'd still take it. Game time.

"Again, I hope this works," she said, and moved her arm like she was pushing a button.

And then we were all in outer space.

Of course we weren't *really*, but when she put space on all the screens on the walls, with planets moving around, it kind of felt like it.

"For this challenge," Science Teacher said, "you will have to reach out quickly to select the right answers. You'll want to move in front of your desks and make sure there's nothing right in front of you at home. I don't want anyone getting hurt."

I checked. I'd be fine.

"I like it," Jasper said. His yellow-suited avatar was right next to me. He stretched his arms a little.

"Yeah," I agreed. "But in that suit, you look more like you want to go for a jog than travel through space."

"I'm better dressed for it than you," he said, pointing at my lacrosse uniform. I guess there weren't too many lacrosse teams in space. Which of course should be fixed. It would be awesome playing lacrosse in zero gravity.

"Some alien might think you're their brother," I said. "Or a giant lemon. And Pink Hair here is strawberry ice cream."

We both laughed, but I don't think either V or Pink did. At least I had Jasper on my team. Hopefully the other two wouldn't slow us down.

"Okay," Teacher Lady said, "this should put each team in a breakout room."

The words *Entering team room* appeared in my goggles.

Then instead of seeing the whole class, it was just the four of us in a smaller room, but still surrounded by space pictures. In the top corner of my vision I saw our team name, JaVaHuDa. So terrible.

"Help whichever member of your team gets this first question," Science Teacher said, her voice intercomming into our room. "Here it is: You know how important the sun is to our lives, but do you know how *big* it is?" The screens changed to a picture of the sun with Mercury, Venus, and Earth orbiting around it. "How many earths could you fit inside the sun?"

Four answers flashed into existence in front of me, and floated there.

All right. I was the member of our team who had to answer the first question. Bring it on.

Each choice was bold and in 3D:

A. 300
B. 1,300
C. 3,100
D. 1,300,000

I had no idea what the answer was.

"I think it's the last one," Daebak said. In a flash, I flung my arm out and slammed it.

Speed!

appeared in front of me.

But did you get it right? . . .

The three dots pulsed, showing that the program was waiting for all the other teams to answer.

A moment later, the top three team names scrolled up into view. JaVaHuDa was tied for first.

"That's what I'm talking about," I said, and clapped a few times.

"Good job, Hunter and Daebak," Vanya said.

"I'm glad you guys knew it," Jasper said. "I had no idea."

"Good," Ms. Teacher said. "It's just crazy to think about how massive our sun is. And we need it to survive." She gave us a few more facts about it, then cleared her throat. "Let's move on."

"Okay," I said, "let's keep it up."

"Question two," Science Teacher said. "What kind of a star is our sun?"

Again, four choices, but they appeared in front of Jasper:

A. Yellow Dwarf

B. Red Giant

C. Protostar

D. Supergiant

"It's got to be Supergiant," I said, and wanted to reach over and slam it.

"I don't think so," Vanya said.

"Daebak?" Jasper said.

"I'm pretty sure it's a yellow dwarf," Daebak said.

That didn't sound right. You could fit over a million earths in it. But Jasper hit *yellow dwarf.*

Then he looked over at me. "Sorry," he said, "he got the last one right."

I wanted to protest, but I really wasn't sure.

The stats came up again and we'd got it right. This time we were in first, no tie.

I didn't want to celebrate that one quite as much, but at least we were in the lead.

"Our sun is a yellow dwarf," Madame Science said. "It's definitely not the biggest of the stars out there. We'll learn more about them and other giant things in the universe. But we'll also learn about the incredibly small." Something appeared, floating in front of each of us, that seemed like we were looking at it through a microscope. "This question is for anyone in your group," she said. "You're looking at a cell. In a way, cells are just as complex as stars and planets. For this question, you will simply touch the right answer." I wasn't sure exactly what that meant, but there were different parts of the cell. "Which part is the nucleus?"

"The center," I said, and slammed the dark circle just off the center.

A moment later, words filled our view. *4 out of 4 got this answer correct.*

"So epic! We're on fire!" Jasper almost yelled. "If there's a trophy, we are going to get it."

And then the questions kept coming, each of us taking turns, or sometimes a couple of us, or all of us. We looked at other parts of the cell. There were questions about plants, tides, and water. We weren't perfect, but we actually did all right together. We would shout out answers, and I think we were pretty fast. We got six questions in a row, then messed up a couple. But only one of those was my fault.

After the last question, we all watched the leader board. We had been in the top two.

And the winner is . . .

JaVaHuDa!

Stupid name, but it was great to see it at the top.

"Yes!" I celebrated.

"Right on," Jasper said. "JaVaHuDa! JaVaHuDa!" He started chanting and the other two joined in. I didn't really want to, but it was kind of fun.

Ms. Science then described how the rest of the semester would go. Not as interesting as the game. I stopped listening after a while. Finally, after forever, class was over.

As we stood up to walk out, Jasper motioned to everyone at the table. "We were pretty epic together," he said. "I can't stop thinking about it."

But then he said something totally stupid. He pointed at Daebak and Vanya. "Do you guys play video games?"

"Yeah," Daebak said, "who doesn't?"

"A little," Vanya said.

I was afraid I knew where this was going. It was like watching a broken play in lacrosse, knowing it was about to end terribly.

"So I'm trying to get ready for that tournament," Jasper said. "Hunter and I have already played together. We're totally going for the trophies!" He said "we." I was in. "Any chance you guys want to join us?"

He wanted them too.

He was inviting these weirdos to come play, just like he had invited me. There was no way they could do what we did in *Infestation*. No way. They would be dead weight.

I had to do something. "They probably don't—" I started.

"I'd love to," Daebak said quickly.

"Yeah," Vanya said.

"Seriously," I said. "Maybe—"

"Sounds great," Jasper cut me off. "Let's meet during free time after lunch."

I wanted to do something, but what? I really wanted to win this tournament, and after playing with a few other guys, I think Jasper's my best shot.

But not these two.

This was not a good move.

CHAPTER 24

THE FURRIEST

Edelsabeth

I filmed us. A good-looking lacrosse player, a rock star, a track kid, and me, Miss Basic, walking down the hall together toward the games. I felt like the odd piece that just didn't fit.

When I edited it into a movie for Mom, I'd say something like, "Hey, Mom," and then I'd sing, "one of these things is not like the other." She'd get the idea. And then I was going to say something like, "to give you the update, I'm now trying really hard to not care what I look like and make friends. I'm trying so hard that I'm going to play VR video games. That's right. Me, Edelsabeth—your daughter—is going to play video games."

She would definitely know I was trying.

I didn't play handheld video games much at all. Like never. I didn't play many other games either. But I was coordinated. So I might be okay at VR. At least, that's what I was hoping. If not, I was going to look incredibly stupid.

Hunter was still scowling. If he knew it was me, everything

would be different. He'd be laughing, glad I was invited. But with Vanilla Vanya, it was clear he thought I didn't have much to offer.

I'm not usually very competitive, but I really wanted to prove him wrong.

But I also wasn't sure that I could.

It was really fun to play the science game with Daebak. Maybe that was a clue to figuring out who he was. He was pretty smart too. When I asked how he knew all that science stuff, he just said, "YouTube videos."

Maybe seeing how he played games would give me more clues about who he really was, and why he liked this version of me better than the real-school version.

"We have to be able to play all the games for the tournament," Jasper said. "I want that trophy," he called out, raising his hand—it was like a battle cry. "So we can do any of them. Vanya, why don't you pick?"

I liked Jasper. He was competitive, like Hunter. But he was also really different; he was giving me and Daebak a chance. And his polyester tracksuit had style.

I could tell Hunter wanted to play the shoot-the-aliens game, and maybe if I was a better undercover friend, or maybe if Hunter had been nicer to me, I would have gone with that. But I would probably do terrible at that game, and then Jasper wouldn't want me on the team, and I wouldn't get to hang out with Daebak more and figure out who he was. And I would miss this chance to maybe even win Hunter back, even without looking like me.

So I looked a little more closely at all the games. There was *SkateCoaster*, a game where you rollerbladed on a roller coaster.

I might be okay at that. Maybe my mountain biking, with leaning into turns and reaction to obstacles, would help. But I didn't want to look stupid. I didn't want to fail.

There was the obstacle course. We'd done that in P.E., and I wasn't terrible. *Creation* had something to do with building. And . . .

"That one," I said, pointing.

Jasper laughed a little. "I think I saw that coming."

"*Seriously?*" Hunter asked, staring at the game.

"A million percent," I said. Maybe I also picked it for a little revenge.

"*The Furriest?*" Hunter asked, reading the 3D title of the game as it rotated in front of us. The letters were made of tufts of fluffy fur in all sorts of patterns: leopard, cheetah, zebra, feathers. We walked in, and a furry start button levitated about chest high. "This isn't a real game," Hunter scoffed. "It looks like a cartoon for five-year-olds. Let's go blast alien spiders again, or try *SkateCoaster.*"

"We have to know how to play this one too," Jasper said. "We might as well give it a shot."

"I'm game," Daebak said.

Was that another clue? He was an amazing looking dancer that was willing to try a game like this? Plus, if I had to guess, he was excited to be here too. I hoped he was. Maybe he even turned down other friends to be here.

"Nah, let's—" Hunter started to say, but then Jasper hit the start button.

Immediately everything went dark and recorded giggles echoed around us. Then a flash of yellow fur ran in front of us, a little too fast to really see. Then green. Then someone opened a virtual door. Light flooded in and we saw cartoony trees with different brightly colored fluffy tops. A stream of purplish water ran through our view with a path that followed it, crossing it with a bridge every so often.

And we saw each other in the game for the first time. We all looked absolutely ridiculous.

Well, both ridiculous and adorable.

In *The Furriest*, everyone's avatar had been converted to a bushy fuzzball with an animal face, like an animal puffed out into a fuzzy sphere. No neck. No body. Just a fluffy sphere with little arms and legs spurting out the sides.

Hunter was a fluff of fur with a bunny face and ears. The fur was red, like his shirt. If nothing else good happened today, this alone was worth it. And when you looked at him, his name, "Hunter," appeared in fuzzy letters right in front of him. I guess they wanted us to be able to tell who was who.

"I totally can't take you seriously looking like that," Jasper said—but his voice was a lot higher than normal, like he'd been breathing helium. "Wait? What?" he said, hearing his own voice. "I sound like a chipmunk before puberty."

"Yeah, you do," Hunter said, then his little bunny face scrunched up as he realized his voice was just as high. Jasper didn't look any better—he had extra-puffy yellow feathers and a duck bill. He was the fluffiest, roundest duck ever.

"This is so weird," Daebak said.

"Said the pink gerbil ball," Hunter said.

"I'm liking the pink," I told Daebak, strangely hearing my higher-pitched voice. And he was like ten levels of adorable.

"Thanks—and you're rocking that mouse look," Daebak said, between laughs. I had to switch my view in the program to see, but I was a blue and white mouse ball.

"Well, thank you," I said in my chipmunk voice.

So far, this was the best thing that had happened at VR school. I loved it. I wasn't pretty. There was no flair or fashion. But for the first time since I was here, I felt a little relief. I didn't stand out as less than everyone else. We were equals. Sure, we looked ridiculous, but I looked just as ridiculous as everyone else.

Large fuzzy numbers flashed above us:

3, 2 . . .

"Looks like we're starting," Jasper said. "Get ready."

"Run as fast as you can," a little narrator voice said, a graphic showing us to move our feet up and down in the real world for our fluffy avatars to run. "Dodge the broken hearts and tears while cheering up the animals in the forest with high fives and hugs." Another diagram showed us how to move side to side with our hands. Doing the high fives and hugs were pretty much the same as in the real world.

1.

Beep.

Giggles.

And then we were all running, our little tiny legs wiggling

and whirling, our weird bodies swaying from side to side as we
sprinted.

I lost it again. We looked hilarious.

"Who made this and why?" Hunter asked, his little furry
body racing forward, veering to the left to avoid a broken heart
that dropped from the sky.

"Some sappy programmer didn't get enough stuffed animals
as a kid," Jasper said. A fuzzy cat poked its head out of the trees
on the side of the path. As Jasper gave it a high five, a cha-ching
sound echoed. Then giggles. I guessed that's how we racked up
points.

"Or maybe they think they can solve the world's problems
with high fives and hugs," Daebak said, dodging two teardrops
that fell.

"Maybe you can," I said. A puffy dog stood in the middle of
the path. Just before I was about to collide with him, I spread my
arms, and we both bounced into a fluffy hug.

Cha-ching. Giggles. Points.

"Ahhhhh," a whole bunch of background voices said.

"I think I just threw up in my mouth a little," Hunter said,
but hearing it in a high voice just made it funny.

"Watch out for the hole in the bridge," Jasper said, as we all
crossed to the other side of what was now a reddish orange river.

Daebak almost fell in.

"Get the cow on the left," I said.

Jasper ran-waddled over and high-fived it.

"I've got the chicken," Hunter said.

"I'll take the pig," Daebak said.

"We are saying the craziest things," I said, panting a little. I think we were all a little out of breath. We were constantly moving our feet up and down and laughing. "This game is genius," I said, moving over to get ready to high-five another puffball, and still laughing.

"This is *not* genius," Hunter said.

"It kind of is," Daebak said.

"Focus, people," Jasper said, coughing to clear his throat. "Sorry," he said, "I have this weird thing where I cough when I exercise sometimes." He moved ahead. "We need more happiness points."

"I still can't take Jasper seriously with that voice," I said. "Or me." I almost slammed right into a broken heart. I hadn't laughed this hard in a long time.

We called out, moving and directing each other. After climbing two mountains, and ending with a race through the clouds, we figured out that if we ran faster and tucked in our heads, our little furry bodies would roll. It was like fuzzy bowling. And if there were candies really high in the air, one of us could run to the other who could bounce us up high to catch it. It was seriously a rush.

We finished the level to cheers, giggles, and more confetti than anyone had ever needed.

"Not bad, guys," Jasper said, still high-pitched and panting. "We do work pretty well together. Let's try again." He stretched his little duck body. "Hunter, focus more on the left side of the road, Vanya likes the right." It was like getting coached by a five-year-old. His words were good, but he was just so cute. "And let's call out when we need a boost."

"Seriously," Hunter said, "we have to do that *again*?"

"That was awesome," Daebak said. "I'm game for round two."

And then he did a dance. It was a slide and a kick, and then a full spin. I'm sure in real life, it was prime time video material, but as a fluffy pink gerbil, it just looked hilarious. A puffball dancer.

I was going to remember this for the rest of my life.

Maybe doing virtual school could work out. Maybe I could show Mom I could figure out life without obsessing about my looks.

Finally something had gone right.

CHAPTER 25
AT THE TABLE

Bradley

"Pass me another of my homemade burritos," Dad said.

"This is my favorite kind of homemade," my mom said, taking another bite. She said something like that anytime it wasn't her turn to make dinner.

"So," my dad said, turning to me, "how goes practice?" He was all smiles. I think he knew the answer.

"Good," I said. Jasper had signed us up to play the tournament together about a week ago, and we'd been practicing almost every day since. I know Hunter wasn't too pleased about it. I think he wanted some superteam of the best players in the school, but Jasper said he likes the way we work together. He said that he and Hunter may be stronger in some games, but Vanya and I are stronger in others. I think Hunter just wants to blast alien spiders, do the obstacle course, and ride *SkateCoaster*. He hates *The Furriest* and *Creation*.

I've been nervous, thinking he'd ask me more questions about

Balderstein Middle School, but he hasn't. I think I'm just not his focus. He hangs out with those girls he met at the orientation party and another friend a lot. And he's still asking about Edelle.

"We don't always get along," I told my dad, "but we actually play pretty well together. Well, as soon as we can get Vanya to quit getting eaten by alien insects." She's done that a few times. I think this whole preparing-for-a-tournament thing is really pushing her. But she's probably one of the best at *The Furriest*; she just loves the whole game. She isn't the fastest, but she gets a ton of points. She's pretty good at *SkateCoaster* too. She has really good balance, leans into turns, always picks the right track, and dodges all the obstacles. I think she's fallen off the least of any of us. And she's great in *Creation*. That's a game where you are given a challenge to build something using various pieces. You have a time limit and have to do the best you can. Except you literally have to carry pieces to the various parts of what you're building. Think Minecraft, but with more exercise. It takes the most teamwork, and Vanya is pretty great as part of a group.

It's just the alien insects that keep throwing her off.

My dad laughed. "Getting eaten by alien insects does sound like a problem."

"Like you could do any better," Mom said. My dad almost never played video games. My mom has played with me every now and then, and she's actually pretty good. She used to help me pass certain levels when I was younger. But not my dad. If he played, it was an exception; and he was always pretty terrible.

"They should have a parent night and let us come play all these games," Dad said. "Then we'd see."

"That would be awesome," I said. "We'd thrash you."

My dad likes to talk big, but just picturing him trying to beat us was pretty funny. Growing up, I could lap him twice in *RaggedRace*. The funny thing is that he didn't even realize it. He still thought he had a chance to win when he passed the finish line. And then he got disappointed.

"Yeah," he admitted, "you'd probably eat my lunch real quick."

Now if I could just get Hunter to leave Vanya alone. Whenever she makes a mistake, he thinks he's team captain and lays into her. I guess he does it to me sometimes too. He needs to relax a little. Jasper gets a little discouraged when we're not playing well, but in general he just keeps giving direction and pointers, and yelling about how he wants that trophy. He seems to really like our team.

"So when's the actual competition?" Mom asked.

"In three weeks," I said, "but we're trying to practice every day to get ready."

"Sounds smart," Mom said, but then she remembered a story from work she wanted to tell my dad. That was my cue to zone out, which was good because I had just received a text.

Yes. It was true.

Let the annals of history show that Bradley Horvath was texting people other than his grandma or his cousins in Reno. *And* he was even texting a person *his age*. "Could that possibly be true?" Boom! Check out the evidence. You can read it on my phone.

Like I have.

Several times a day, every conversation, over and over again.

Daebak is so much better than Bradley was.

Vanya had asked to trade numbers a few days ago so we could coordinate videos and practice times and stuff. But we have mostly just been chatting. Jasper gathered everyone's numbers the next day to set up a group chat so we'd show up to practice at the same time. We message each other through the school's MeetUp, but we're not always on at night when we need to decide things. So we've been texting tips and when to meet and where.

What's the weirdest though is that when Jasper asked for numbers, Vanya gave him a different phone number than the one she gave me. I have no idea why. But it made me feel like she gave me her personal number because we were that good of friends.

Vanya:

> Good call choosing *The Furriest* again today.

Me:

> Thanks. Anytime Hunter's a waddling bunny it's a good day.

Vanya:

> Right? That should be his avatar.

A little laugh slipped out. I looked up at my parents, but they were still talking about work.

Then Vanya texted a picture of Hunter racing with his little determined bunny face all scrunched up.

This time I couldn't hold my laugh in at all. It just burst out of me. And I didn't look up at my parents because I didn't want it to be all awkward.

Me:

> That's a total wallpaper.

She had posted a few pics of herself playing *The Furriest* and *SkateCoaster* on MeetUp and talked about the tournament. I always checked them out and liked them, though not enough other people seemed to.

And she's posted a few more dance videos of me. She seems to really like it and keeps telling me that I'm good at it. But she's a wizard at making me look amazing. You better believe I watch every one of them, but I like reading what she says more. *Another video of my friend Daebak. The kid's got talent.*

It's like the best evidence that my life is different. People know me, they think I've got talent, and someone even publicly called me their friend. This was working.

Daebak: The Movie. It was going to happen one day.

Vanya:

> What about this one?

She sent another picture—me blasting an alien spider. And I looked good, like movie-poster epic. Except my face looked absolutely terrified. (Scratch the whole movie poster thing.) Apparently I make weird faces when I'm under stress. It looked like I'd just eaten a booger-flavored jelly bean.

Me:

> Wow, just wow. I'm surprised I can't just scare off the aliens with that face.

Vanya:

 I like it. It's adorable.

I read that text again.

And again.

I may have even screenshotted it.

Vanya posted about other people too. She had videos of Jasper that made him look absolutely amazing. She had posted nice things about others in her classes. She rocked a video of Hunter on *SkateCoaster* that made him look like a superhero. I would have never done that. She just seems to keep trying to be nice to that guy. No idea why.

I posted some of Vanya's pics on my social media too. I got a decent response; Jasper, Vanya, Jordan, Keiko, and lots of people I didn't really know follow. Keiko commented with stuff like "Weird" or "Stand up for alien spider rights!"

I have actually hung out with Keiko a little too. Nothing big, just one day I invited her to hang out with Vanya and me after making a dance video. She's pretty cool.

"Bradley?" Mom asked.

"What?" I said, looking up.

"Your mom just asked you a question," Dad said.

"Oh, sorry," I said. "I didn't hear. What did you ask?"

"I asked what you were laughing at," she said. "But now, I want to know why you're smiling."

"Sorry," I said, maybe blushing a little. "It's just my friend's texts are pretty great."

"What did we say about texting at dinner?" Dad asked,

furrowing his brow, his voice getting deeper. There were probably about a bazillion dads asking the same question throughout the world. My parents also knew and could quote at will all the statistics and studies about how family dinner time was important for raising emotionally stable youth.

"You said it was okay," I said.

"I know," Dad said, dropping the scowl. "I just wanted to seem like an angry dad for a second. Did I pull it off? Were you afraid?"

"An attempt was made," I said. He was about as good at getting angry as he was with video games. My parents said that they might not always let me text at dinner, but for now it was allowed. I still couldn't watch videos or shows or listen to music during dinner, but they really didn't mind if I texted my friends. I think they might have been almost as excited about it as I was.

Vanya:

> I'm really nervous about the
> practice game tomorrow.

The school had let us sign up to play some games against another team. After practice for a week, it would be a good opportunity to see if we were any good.

Me:

> You'll do great.

Though I was a little nervous too.

I hoped I could do virtual school forever. I had friends. I was getting invited to things. I was even dancing. This was everything I wanted. As long as I could keep Hunter from not always freaking out at Vanya—or finding out who I really was—I think my life would be absolutely perfect.

"Still texting?" Dad asked.

"Kind of," I said.

"Keep it up," Dad said. "I'll start on your dishes."

I bet no other kid in the world has heard their dad say that.

CHAPTER 26
SKATECOASTER

Edelsabeth

I raced down the track, my skates spinning at what felt like a hundred miles an hour. There was no way I could go this fast in real life.

But right now I was just trying to not look absolutely stupid again.

"Okay, guys," Hunter said, "we've got to make up some points. Focus."

I was the reason we had to make up points. We were in a practice game: JaVaHuDa against the Killer Monkeys. I'm not sure where they got that name, but so far, they *had* been pretty killer. For the practice match we were only going to play three games. The first was *Creation*. We had to make a building that could withstand an earthquake. Daebak was really smart about choosing the right blocks for the foundation, and I'm really good at staying organized and focused and helping us build together.

Jasper says that I should take over as coach on that game, and for Hunter to be quiet and just do what I say.

That's one of my favorite games right now, for obvious reasons.

We finished the building within the time limit, and it withstood ten more seconds of earthquake than the Killer Monkeys' building did. We were up by 16 points.

But then we played *Infestation*. That's definitely not my favorite. I may or may not scream when certain alien insect monsters jump out at me.

And this time, I screamed and shot in the wrong direction right before I died. I could hear the people who had come to watch the games laughing. I'm still hoping no one was recording it. I already had enough problems getting noticed without that being posted everywhere.

But after I was gone, that left my team with only three people, and they didn't get nearly as far in the game as the Killer Monkeys. That left us down 19 points, and Hunter was on a bit of a rampage. I think he's extra mad because the Monkeys have Ruby on their team, the girl he likes to hang out with. I know he would have loved to have her on our team if Jasper hadn't invited Daebak and me. I also think Grace, the other girl he hangs out with, was watching.

Hunter pulled me aside and told me that I had to focus and carry my weight, totally forgetting all the good I did in the first game. But here's the kicker: Ruby died only a minute after me. I heard him talking to Ruby between games and he was so nice to her: "Yeah, that happens sometimes." It was like if you're cute, you're not expected to do as much. You get a few more free passes. But if you're not, you have to earn them.

So now I was skating the best I possibly could.

Following the track, I leaned left, then right, then tucked in for a crazy drop. I'm not even sure I'd be able to survive a drop like this in real life.

I was currently in second place, behind the Monkeys' best player.

I had to catch him.

If I did, the crowd could take videos of that and post it. I'd be fine with that. And then maybe Hunter would calm down.

In various places, the track would split into two to five different tracks. You had to pick one, but later, they all came back together. Some of the tracks were better than others, though. The trick was to try to catch a glimpse of what was beyond the split in the fraction of a second you had to choose.

I was pretty good at that.

As I flew down the hill, I could tell the track would branch out into three. On the far right was a high jump. You fly high, and can get extra points for tricks and can grab coins for more points. Most of the boys would go that way, but it was a bit of a trap. Sure, you got coins and could show off, but it cost you time. You got more points for finishing fast. Only pick jumps that send you far, not high.

One of the tracks broke off into a winding path. No good. All the turns slow you down.

One of the paths was flat and straight, but had obstacles you had to dodge. That one was mine.

The boy in front of me took the jump.

This was my chance.

I shot down the path, lifting my left foot, then right, jumping, dodging the junk on the track. It felt a little like mountain biking, veering to dodge rocks, or big dips in the path.

The boy was doing fancy tricks in the air, and I was passing him.

"You've got this," I heard Daebak yell behind me. He'd taken the same path. He says he does better when he just follows me.

I jumped, then tucked in more. That was risky; with a bigger tuck, sometimes it was hard to jump and move. But I had this. I had to get those points back.

I could see the finish line up ahead, just a little past the point the tracks came back together.

Out of the corner of my eye, I saw the boy on the other team land. I was ahead. This was going to work.

I tucked further. Just two more obstacles to miss. I leaned left, then . . .

Whoa, there were two more obstacles behind a bigger one. I had lifted my right foot, but couldn't bring it down yet, or I would hit an obstacle. I was falling off balance. I was going to nose-dive and scream and crash in front of everyone watching.

My right leg had to come down, but in order to try to miss the obstacle, I tried to place it further forward, stretching it out front. It worked, but then I was so off balance I veered to one side and then the other.

"Whoa," Daebak said, "hang in there."

It was too much. My legs moved into the splits and I crashed in what had to be the absolute most ungraceful way. Screeching and tumbling, my legs in weird directions.

"Oh," Daebak said, watching me topple, "stay down for a sec." I taught him that. I had leapt over him a few times in practice. He cleared me.

I got up as fast as I could, moved my feet to get back momentum, but by the time I hit the finish line, I was in fifth. Just like that I went from almost winning to the bottom half.

Ruby had beaten me, and I looked absolutely terrible in the process.

CHAPTER 27

AN IDEA

Hunter

I was smiling on the outside, furious on the inside. Vanya had it in the bag and she messed it up.

"Good try," Ruby said, smiling. We were walking to the commons to hang out after the practice game.

"You and Jasper got really high scores," Grace said.

That part felt good. It wasn't lacrosse, but it did have a crowd, and Grace was there, seeing me give it my best. When she and the others who came to watch were in the viewer room, I could decide if I wanted them to appear in a box in the corner of my view. I could also decide if I wanted to hear their cheers. I definitely chose both. I was back to playing in front of a crowd. That was a piece of me I really needed.

And it was really fun to play against Ruby, though I hated losing.

Especially since I had another bald spot developing. Well, that's not the right word. It pretty much just showed up, totally uninvited. Hair there, then a day and a half later, another quarter-sized bald spot. This one was on the side of my head by my ear, another tough spot to cover up. That day I screamed and punched my wall and ran faster than Ryker on our run.

Last night I woke up and couldn't go back to sleep.

I had to focus.

The team. The tournament. This was one thing I thought I could control. But in the practice game we totally came up short.

"Daebak is really cute," Grace said. "But he makes some pretty funny faces in *Infestation*."

I'm glad she added that last part. I'd seen Grace talk to him a few times and didn't know what I thought about that. It was another reason it was great to have them watch us; I'd saved Daebak like four times.

Ruby checked over her shoulder. "Vanya could use a little work," she added. She was smart to make sure the team wasn't following.

"Right?" I said. Jasper and I were almost breaking records in *Infestation* when Vanya died. Daebak was doing okay. But unless Vanya could shape up, more teams would beat us.

Vanya was nice enough, I guess. She even posted a video of me the other day. I looked awesome—and I totally saved it—but it felt weird. Like either she was trying to get me to lay off her when she made mistakes, or like she was trying to become more popular by being on a team with me.

"I'll take her place," Ruby said.

"That would be awesome," I said, and gave her a high ten. You don't know how much I liked that idea. That would change everything. I still loved the practice, the goal, something to excel at. But if I could do it with someone like Ruby, all the better. "Let's play together sometime."

"Sure," she said, "I'd love it."

That felt good. Just asking a bold question and getting a positive answer. Like before the pandemic and before stupid bald spots, when I could try to make the most of life and be excited about what was happening.

"Not me," Grace said. "You two can have it. I'm not much of a gamer."

I respected her answer. I thought it might be what Edelle would say. She wasn't into games much either.

"Vanya isn't a gamer either," Ruby said.

"That's the problem," I added. She was trying, but she didn't have the drive.

I'd been spending more time with Grace and Ruby and a guy named Landon I met in math. It felt a little more like my old friend group. A lot of talking, jokes, a little flirting. It's been pretty great.

"Are you sure you're not Edelle?" I asked Grace. There were other ways she reminded me of her. The tan skin, she laughed at what I said, she had a nice sense of style. She's shy, but she's not really.

By her reaction, I think she would have blushed if the program could show it. "Maybe," she said.

Ever since I told her about Edelle, she has teased me that she's really her. So of course I tried to quiz her—I asked about what shake I used to order when we got together as friends, what Fetu was like, and what happened at some of my lacrosse games. She always avoided the questions, saying things like, "You know," and "I think that answer's pretty obvious." I was pretty sure she was just pretending to be Edelle, but there was a chance. And I had searched the whole school and I hadn't found anyone else who was more like her.

"Good job today," Jasper said to me, catching me from behind. He cleared his throat, then turned to the girls. "You too," he said, pointing at Ruby.

"Hey, Jasper," Ruby said. I think she had been flirting a little with him too. Not as much as she flirted with Daebak and definitely not as much as she flirted with me. I guess that was okay. Jasper was definitely cool enough, but the bright yellow tracksuit? Still a little strange.

"We just had an idea," I told Jasper. "What if we let Ruby try out for our team?" I kind of wanted to say that we should kick Vanya off and put Ruby in instead, but I opted for the nicer way. "And if you like the way she plays we could see if we can change rosters."

Jasper shifted his mouth as he thought about it. "I'd love to play with Ruby," Jasper said, "but we've got our team."

"But," I said, "what if we talk to Vanya; she isn't that great at some of the games. Maybe she'll let us switch out her spot. Maybe that would even be a relief for her."

"I think she's great," Jasper said. "Sure, she turfs it sometimes, but she's getting better. And she's awesome at *Creation*, *The Furriest*, and usually rocks *SkateCoaster*."

"She doesn't rock *Infestation*," I said.

"I'll give you that," Jasper said. "We need her to stay alive in there a little longer."

"You could let Ruby play with us just once to see if she's better," I said. "And if she is . . ." I let the thought hang there.

Jasper shook his head and cleared his throat again. "I got kicked off a soccer team once," he said. "I hated it. Like *really* hated it. There is no way I'm doing that to anyone else. The team's set."

I couldn't imagine anyone kicking Jasper off a team. He's amazing.

"Plus," he said, "if I remember the rules, we can't make changes unless one of us can't play, and then we can only pick up someone who's not signed up on another team." He started walking faster down the hall. I guess that was his way of saying that his mind was made up.

"We could ask," I called after him. "Please?"

He laughed and kept walking to class.

"It was a good try," Ruby said. "Thanks."

She saw that I fought for her. That felt good. Some guys wouldn't have even tried that.

I heard a noise and glanced back. Vanya and Daebak were walking right behind us. Daebak was glaring at me. Vanya was looking at the ground.

How long had they been there?

CHAPTER 28

ANNOUNCEMENT

Edelsabeth

I heard the whole thing.

The whole thing.

It was the next morning, and I still couldn't stop thinking about it.

I'd been trying to become friends with him. I was trying to win him over with a generic avatar that didn't look much like me. I'd been friendly. I'd talked to him. I'd posted a video of him and complimented him.

And he responded like that.

If my feelings were a person, they'd be rocking that fiery crimson dress again and steel-toed boots and a lightning pitchfork. I was angrier with Hunter than I had been with Mom when this whole thing started.

If Hunter knew it was really me, he would fight for me to be on the team, not to kick me off. He wouldn't want to replace me with Ruby.

And now he was sitting right across from me in science.

I didn't know everything Mom wanted me to learn at the virtual school, but right now I was infuriated at how easily someone could mess everything up because I didn't look like I used to.

I appreciated how Jasper had stuck up for me. For some reason, he thinks that I can do it, that I have something I bring to the team. Daebak, too. I always feel a little uncomfortable when we play, but he's always pointing out when I do things well.

But not Hunter.

I looked over at him and he was talking to Jasper about the game. He was purposefully not making eye contact because he didn't know how much I knew. Or he could sense my fury. These VR sets need an option for me to shoot death lasers at him.

BRRRRRIIIINGGG

The bell rang, then immediately after, Mila Holota, the woman in charge of NovaMillennium, appeared at the front of our room. Of course, she was probably appearing in all the rooms across the school. Ms. Allen was still at her desk.

"Hello, everyone," Mila said and nodded. "Thank you for your great work in school. Your attendance is way up over both online *and* traditional school, which we are really excited about. Thanks so much for participating. We're only three weeks away from our first-ever VR games tournament." A few people clapped. Hunter would probably have whooped and cheered, but he was quieter than usual. "And we have another announcement."

Another one? What else could she say? Please tell me that they're banning Hunter Athanasopoulos from the game tournament for totally overlooking one of his best friends and trying to kick her off his team.

"This," Mila continued, "will actually happen the weekend before the tournament. You don't have to form teams or practice. Just come and have a great time." She raised a finger to correct herself. "Well, I guess you can practice if you'd like." She took a few steps forward. "In two weeks," she said, "on Wednesday night, we will have our first ever . . ." She paused for effect. "Virtual . . . *reality . . . DANCE!*" She raised both hands. It was as excitable as the ever-professional Mila got.

Immediately almost everyone started mumbling.

A dance.

Part of me loved that idea, but I was still really mad at Hunter, and I didn't want to be distracted from my anger.

Hunter started clapping. "All right," he said, back to his normal self. "The kids at real schools don't even get those."

He made a good point. We had a chance for fun that other people didn't have. Pandemic numbers were too high for crowded dances, even with masks.

I'd only been to two dances. Back in Houston we'd had a dance in fifth grade where we had to do the waltz and other formal dances we had learned in class. We even had dance cards. It was kind of fun, everyone overthinking who they'd ask for which dance, and everyone guessing who liked who. When the actual dance was over, I felt all fuzzy inside, like I was more mature, one step closer to being a full-grown adult.

Then last year in sixth grade, we were supposed to have two dances. I was so excited for the first one at the end of the semester. I had started getting a lot of attention on the website and at school, and I was nervous that the dance could make or break me. I had a couple small meltdowns, first trying to find the perfect dress, and then when my hair wouldn't cooperate. Once I got there it wasn't Cinderella-perfect, but it was pretty great. I was asked to dance every dance. And Hunter asked me twice. That was one of the first times we hung out.

The second dance was canceled because of the pandemic.

I definitely didn't want to dance with Hunter at this next one.

I glanced over at Daebak and he was looking at me, like he was trying to check if I was all right. I gave him as much of a smile as I could manage. We'd texted all about it last night, but I was still upset.

Ms. Allen started class, but it was incredibly hard to pay attention to outer space facts with all that had happened yesterday with Hunter and then the dance announcement on top of it. But I think it all built to the moment I got a text. I was hoping it would be something funny or cute from Daebak or Jasper to calm me down, or distract me. But no.

Hunter:

> A dance, Edelle. Let's meet up at the dance!!!!!

I wanted to reach over and slap him. The day after he tried to kick me off a team to replace me with another girl, *he invited me to the dance*. I could barely think straight.

But somehow one idea popped into my head. It was the best response to what he'd done. It would just have to wait until the end of class.

Finally the bell rang, and I looked across the table.

"Hey, Hunter," I said.

"Yeah?" he said, smiling a bit bigger than before.

It was all building up inside me. He just didn't get it. He wasn't treating me like *me* at all. And I was tired of it.

"I'm Edelle," I said.

CHAPTER 29

TRUTH

Edelsabeth

Hunter just stared at me for a second. I could see his mind working. He was making connections. He was going to put it all together and get hit with a huge wave of guilt, like a tsunami that could take down entire cities. Then he'd spend the rest of the day apologizing. And the rest of the week. And the rest of the semester. And sometime in there we might get on that zoom chat we'd been trying to plan with Fetu and Kennedy, and I'd tell them every embarrassing detail and just watch him squirm.

I didn't have to win him over. He just had to realize that something awesome had been right in front of him the whole time.

He smirked. "No, you're not." He stood up from the table to leave.

"What?" I said, standing too.

"You're not her," he said.

"Yes, I am," I said.

He shook his head. "Nice try. Edelle isn't anything like you."

What? He honestly didn't think I was me.

He shook his head again. "She doesn't look like you. She doesn't dress like you. She doesn't act like you. She wouldn't compete in video games."

I opened my mouth to answer, but was still thinking about what he said. He was right about everything but acting like myself. Right? I was still acting like me. I *was* me. I mean, all of this school and avatar stuff was pretty odd, so I may have been a *little* different. But still me, right?

"I'm her," I finally said.

"This is just you trying to get me to like you," he said. "And it's kind of mean."

"Hey," Daebak said, standing up, "calm down." But Daebak looked a little nervous.

I thought about proving I was her. I could read him the texts he'd sent only to me. I could tell him where we went with all our friends after his lacrosse win. I could tell him that my mom was Palestinian, and that my dog's name is Keniv. There were lots of ways I could do it. But my mind was still reeling, and everyone kept talking.

"Wait," Jasper said, "are you serious? Are you really the girl he's been looking for the whole time, and you were here right under his nose?"

I nodded.

"That's crazy," Jasper said.

"It's *not her*," Hunter insisted, his voice rising. "You guys don't know her, but Edelle is sweet and funny and awesome, and kind of shy."

"Sounds like Vanya to me," Jasper said.

"He's got a point," Daebak said, his face still in a glazed expression.

"*No!*" Hunter said. "Vanya is just trying to get even with me." He looked at me. "You're cool and all, but you're not Edelle. Grace is like twenty times more like Edelle than you."

What? I didn't know Grace very well, and I did see a few similarities, mostly physical, but I didn't want to be compared to her. She followed Hunter around and laughed at every dumb thing that he said. She agreed with everyone about everything. I had never been that way.

Had I?

"Is everything all right here?" Ms. Allen asked. She must have noticed all the commotion.

No, everything was definitely not all right.

CHAPTER 30

WHAT IF . . .

Bradley

My brain was overloading.

Like it could explode or melt into a strange unrecognizable mess.

But I caught up with Vanya in the hall and forced myself to focus on the most important question. "Hey, are you okay? What Hunter did wasn't cool."

She didn't look at me; she just kept walking straight toward her next class. "I'm fine."

She definitely didn't seem fine.

"Hunter's a jerk sometimes," I said. "If he somehow kicks you off the team, I'll go with you. We'll make our own team." I totally meant that. "VaDa. It's not as catchy, but hopefully we'll find more people."

She took several more steps without answering. "Thanks," she said, and then I heard a sniffle.

"Let's get Jasper too," I said. "On our new team, I mean. He's awesome."

That cracked her serious stare just a little and a hint of a smile slivered in. "That's basically just kicking Hunter off."

"Oh, yeah," I said. "I guess so. So maybe let's just do that. Then he'd be on a different team and maybe we'd face them in the tournament, and I could accidentally sic an alien spider on him."

A little more of a smile.

But my brain had been overloaded and weighed down with a bigger question. And I couldn't hold it in. Like a volcano, or a supernova, it was going to have to explode out of me sometime. "Are you *really* Edelle?" I asked, then couldn't help but stare at her, waiting for the answer.

She couldn't be, could she?

She didn't seem like Edelle.

Especially after all of this time with Hunter asking about her and her not saying anything.

Her smile was gone.

She shrugged and shook her head a little. "I was just really mad at Hunter. Like can't-see-straight mad."

Relief. Total relief.

"I would be too," I said as we kept walking. "I still *am*." He was basically tearing apart one of the best things in my life, and doing it by hurting my best friend.

We walked a little more with fewer and fewer people still in the halls. We'd been late getting out of class because of what Vanya had said to Hunter, and now it had to be getting close to the bell, but right now, I didn't really care if I was late to my next class.

"But you know Edelle, right?" Vanya asked. I nodded. "Hunter doesn't think I'm even like her. What do you think?"

The bell rang, echoing through the halls.

That felt like my brain after all the stress since the game yesterday.

I shook my head. "I don't think so either." We were practically alone in the hall.

"Why?" she asked, looking over at me.

Why did she want to know this? Did she really want to be like Edelle because she wanted Hunter's attention, wanted him to like her? Wanted to be the type of girl that a guy like him was searching for, asking everyone about?

"Well," I said, "Edelle was new at my school last year, and when she was there at first, she would talk to me. It wasn't anything big, but she'd ask how I was doing, or what my last class was. And it was really good. I liked it." I could have said that most people didn't pay attention to me or didn't talk to me, but I left that out. "But then she changed," I said. "She made a lot of friends and got a lot of attention, and she didn't talk to me anymore." I paused just a little. "She didn't even notice me. Except when other people laughed at me, and she laughed too."

Vanya just stood there for a moment. "I'm sorry," she finally said.

"It's okay," I said. "We were even going to be partners once for this history project, and she got up and asked the teacher if he would change us so she could work with someone else."

Vanya didn't say anything. Like she was waiting for me to keep talking.

"And this one time in the computer lab," I said, "one of her friends asked Marie Holland for some help, and when she left, Edelle got on Marie's computer. And the next day everyone was talking about how Marie had really ugly pictures of her posted on Parker's site. I guess Marie had been getting closer to the top of 'the list.' But the pictures were of her all sweaty after the mile run, and her making a really ugly face doing sit-ups, and a picture of her tummy poking over her jeans. And then people started calling her Marie Muffin Top. So mean. I was so glad then that I wasn't being rated on a website. I hate rumors, so I didn't say anything, but I think Edelle got the pictures somehow, maybe she even took them, and sent them to Parker from Marie's email."

I looked over at Vanya.

"That's why I don't think you're like her. And I don't think you should be," I quickly added. "You never ignore me. You don't ignore anyone. You don't try to get away from me. You don't send mean pictures of other people. You're the exact opposite," I said. "*Exact opposite*. You spend a lot of time making awesome videos of me, and of Jasper, and other people, even Hunter. You make us look good, feel good." Maybe a little emotion was sliding into my voice. "I can dance in front of you, no problem." I paused. "You make me feel like a rock star." My voice cracked. Not exactly the most rock-star-sounding thing. "Or at least like I could be. And you're . . ."

It didn't quite come out. But I thought of how my life had changed. How I was dancing in the halls sometimes. How I was going to play in a video game tournament, with a team of mostly friends. How I was really excited for a dance. A lot of it had to do with Vanya. I tried again. "You're the best friend I've had in a long time."

There may have been a little moisture in my eyes. And I may have tried to wipe it away, and forgot that I was wearing a huge VR headset. Again.

Vanya gave a half smile, then didn't, and then did. "I'm *not* like her, am I?"

I smiled, but I wasn't sure that was a complete answer.

She pointed down the hall. "I've got to go." And she turned and left as the bell rang.

CHAPTER 31

IN MY BLANKET

Edelsabeth

I curled up on my bed and bawled. I grabbed my blanket, but pushed my unicorn plushie off my bed. She looked too happy.

Nothing was going right. Not with Hunter. Not with Daebak.

I had been trying to prove to Mom that I wasn't obsessed with my looks. That I had all the good stuff that I needed inside. And for a while there, I thought I was doing pretty well.

Not anymore.

Daebak nailed the Marie story. I didn't know that anyone knew. I'd only told Mom after she found the pictures on my phone and interrogated me. I had to send an apology—but I still kept it anonymous.

And just to make me feel even worse, I still didn't know who Daebak was. Everything he said sounded familiar, and I had a couple of ideas, but I still didn't know exactly who.

I found my yearbook and started looking through pictures again, wiping my eyes so they wouldn't drip on the pages.

He had every right not to like Edelle.

Was I any better now? I couldn't even remember who he was.

I heard my door creak open and wanted to pull the blanket over my head. The last thing that I needed was a lecture from Mom.

But it wasn't Mom. A tiny body lifted itself up onto my bed and snuggled in.

Eva wiped my face with her little fingers. "Why are you sad?" Her inflection was so sweet. She even frowned to fit my mood, but I still wasn't in the mood to smile. "Sad. Sad," she repeated herself.

"I wasn't very nice," I said.

"Oh," she said, thinking for a moment. Then her eyes went wide. "Once I wasn't nice because I stole Mom's chocolates." She carefully said each syllable: cha-ko-lates. And her puckering frown switched to a massive smile. "Cha-ko-lates," she repeated.

This time, I laughed, though the tears kept coming.

"You can laugh *and* cry at the same time?" she asked, confused.

I nodded. She wiped my face again. "Want me to get you chocolates?" She moved her hands against each other, like a little conniving villain, but she didn't have the dexterity to do it like in the movies. "They make everyone happy," she said, still smiling. "Except Mom when she finds you with 'em." Her smiled dropped.

I laughed again, but shook my head. I wished chocolates

could fix this. "I'm okay," I said. It wasn't really true, but what else do you tell a three-year-old?

"Stop crying," she said. She didn't know what to do with her wet fingers so she started using my sleeve as a towel. "You're so smart and so nice and so pretty and . . ."

Her attempts to cheer me up didn't help.

Maybe sometimes I was more pretty than nice.

She pushed her hands together again, her eyes wide like she'd just had an amazing idea. "Cha-ko-lates," she said, giving a huge toothy grin, then ran off.

I grabbed the yearbook and kept looking.

CHAPTER 32

KEIKO

Bradley

"How's it going, Keiko?" I asked.

"Whatever," Keiko said flatly, no change in her facial expression. Vanya, Keiko, and I were in the commons during free time.

"Are you excited for the dance?" I asked.

Keiko turned and stared at me. "Guess."

"I'm going to take that as you're secretly excited on the inside," I said.

Vanya smiled at that, which was good. She definitely seemed distracted since her whole claiming-to-be-Edelle thing yesterday. I mean, Hunter had pretty much tried to get her kicked off the team, but it had been a strange reaction to claim to be the girl he'd been trying to find for a while now.

Then again, I guess I know what it's like to want to be someone else.

"I think *you're* excited for the dance, Daebak," Vanya told me, coming out of her haze. She smiled just as big, but seemed to look at me a little different.

"Definitely," I said. And I did a quick shift kick. I was out-of-my-mind *ecstatic* for the dance. Me as Daebak—with friends—laughing and moving to the beat. Especially after the videos Vanya had made and posted. People had messaged me, saying they were excited to see me dance live. Maybe they would even watch me and copy my moves. In this avatar, a dance was practically my Super Bowl, my Emmys, my world tour.

I'd never been to a dance before. The last one got canceled because of the pandemic, but I wouldn't have gone anyway. In fact, there was no amount of money you could have given me to get me to go. (Okay, that might not be true. Anything over six figures *might* have been worth putting the big awkward kid on display and hearing the whispers about peeing my pants. But seven figures? I would totally do it. Then I could move to an island, pay a private tutor, and watch all the YouTube I wanted.)

But that was Bradley. I wasn't him, not here. Here I was Daebak—and I had style and moves, an amazing combination. I could almost guarantee that I was going to be practicing all week so I could bring my prime time material. This would be a pop star in the spotlight. This was my chance, my bop.

Like a mystic chosen warrior, it was like I'd been preparing for this all my life.

Part of me was still kind of scared that the past few days were going to mess everything up, like annihilate it with lasers and a dragon war. For a while it looked like our team was going to completely tear apart, and all my friends would scatter, and the dance would be a total mess. But now it seemed like it might still be okay. Jasper was talking to Hunter, trying to smooth things over. He had talked with me and Vanya, and we both agreed that if Hunter apologized we would give it another shot. If Jasper hadn't wanted it so badly and asked us over and over, I'm not sure what we would have done, but we trusted him and so we gave in. Jasper seemed thrilled that we'd probably be able to patch things up.

But it was still a bit stressful. I was hoping that focusing on the dance might get Vanya excited. And it would be really cool if Keiko came too.

"What if," I said, "we learned a dance together, but we keep it a total secret? Then at the dance, we could all break out our moves totally in sync." I modeled a few possibilities; they just came out of me. "And maybe other people would join in, like one of those flash mobs." I did an arm wrap move over my head as another possible example. I always thought that looked really cool in groups. "It could take over the whole dance." There is no way I would have even *thought* that in school before this, ever.

Vanya smiled. "Awesome."

"No way," Keiko said. "Not if you gave me a new car, a hot tub, and a mile-long rope of licorice."

I looked at Vanya, who shrugged.

"Red licorice," Keiko clarified. "Not black. No one would do anything for black licorice."

"We could make it into a video," I said, looking back at Vanya. "Using your awesome videographer skills, of course. And maybe I should film *you* for part of this one." I really liked that idea, but she never wanted to. She said her place was behind the camera.

I wish Vanya was more excited. And I wish Keiko would at least think more about coming.

Vanya nodded. "There will be a lot of cute boys there," she said. It was awesome that Vanya was trying to help persuade Keiko. Maybe trying to get someone else excited for the dance would get her more excited too.

"I've seen them, you know. Those 'cute' boys," Keiko said.

"You can hang out with us," I said. "I promise we'll make it fun." And I would. I would at least try really hard, anyway.

Her only reaction was rolling her eyes.

Then Jasper walked up. "I'll be there," he said. "*That's* a good reason." Apparently he had finished talking to Hunter and heard what we'd been saying.

"I'm not going," Keiko said, but quieter than before. Jasper knew her from science class too. I think he'd even done a speed chat with her.

"You *have* to come," I said.

"No, I don't," Keiko said. "That's what *non*-mandatory means. Plus, I'm a total introvert, so I have a blanket and a movie calling my name for that night."

I would have thought the same thing a few weeks ago, but for some reason I couldn't picture Keiko snuggled up in a blanket watching a movie.

"The blanket and movie are calling your name already?" Jasper asked with a smile. "The dance is two weeks away."

"Blankets and movies plan well in advance," Keiko said like she was saying something completely normal. "I already have an invitation—and I can't break that commitment." She shook her head, one of her few outward expressions. Like the old Bradley, she probably thought a dance sounded like torture, like the evil netherworld coming up to haunt our dreams with zombies, demons, and streamers.

"Oh, I respect that blanket and movie combination," Vanya said. "But please?"

"No," Keiko said. "Dances are awful. They're always awkward."

"They don't *have* to be," Vanya said. This seemed to be working a little. I loved that Vanya would help me try to persuade Keiko. "It would be more fun if all of our friends could be there."

Keiko responded, "It's just everyone trying to look all pretty and impressive for everyone else—and then they're all too scared to ask anyone else to dance."

Jasper laughed. "That *is* kind of true," he said. "At my school's last dance, they played like five songs before anyone actually started to dance. No one wants to be the first and look stupid."

"Or they *are* stupid and just don't want others to find out," Keiko said.

"I'm going with Jasper's answer," Vanya said.

"Of course, you don't have to come," Jasper said, turning to Keiko. "Your call, but it would be awesome if you did." I loved that he just joined in. He was pretty good at inviting people to stuff. I couldn't quite pin down what it was, but the way he asked you, you wanted to hang out, to give it a shot.

"Probably not," Keiko said.

After a moment, Jasper's eyes went wide. "You said *probably*. That means there's a chance."

"It *doesn't* mean that," Keiko said, her voice actually a little louder than normal.

"What would it take?" Vanya asked.

"What?" Keiko asked.

"What would it take for you to come?" Vanya asked.

"Probably a secret choreographed dance number we all learn together," I said. And yes, I danced again. Jasper loved the idea and danced with me. Someone in the hall saw us and cheered a little. That really was a good idea.

"Definitely not ever," Keiko said. "Ever. Ever. Ever. Ever. Ever. Ever. Ever. Ever." She said like twenty *evers* before having to take a breath.

"That was a lot of evers," I said.

"Ever. Ever. Ever. Ever," she continued. "Ever. Ever."

"And . . . we're back," Jasper said, disappointed.

"Seriously," Vanya said, "what would it take?"

Keiko didn't talk for a second, and then she launched in. She held up a finger. "For it not to be stupid," she said. She held up a second finger. "For people not to care so much about everyone else." And then she actually moved like she was dancing, but deliberately trying to look stupid at the same time, throwing her head in weird directions and moving her arms like spaghetti noodles.

She held up a third finger. "No one caring if you're weird," she said.

No one said a thing.

"And," she added, holding up a fourth finger, "I'd want a *really* long string of licorice."

I looked at Vanya, then Jasper.

"Red," Keiko said. "*Not* black."

Vanya turned to Keiko. "In that case, you've got to try something with me."

"I'm not going to the dance," Keiko said.

"It's not that," Vanya said. "It's something else. Something where no one will care how weird they look."

"I'm a little interested," Keiko said, with only the slightest hint of expression.

"For Keiko that's practically jumping up and down," Jasper said.

"Shut up," she said, punching him in the arm.

"Ow," Jasper said. "I get it. I crossed a line. Sorry."

"Follow me," Vanya said, and we started to walk down the hall. Vanya was full-on doing everything she could to persuade Keiko, but I didn't really know what her plan was.

"Where are we going?" I whispered.

"Sometimes," Vanya said, "in order to not care about how we look, we all have to look the same."

And suddenly I knew.

This was either going to be awesome and hilarious—or a total train wreck.

No. A train wreck on top of a plane crash on a freeway full of car pileups.

Over a sinkhole.

Where the earth is imploding. And a forty-foot tsunami is coming in from one side and a tornado from the other.

CHAPTER 33

ONE MORE THING

Edelsabeth

I looked up as I took a bite of my falafel kemaj.

"How's it going this week?" Mom asked.

I didn't answer. I was still chewing.

"Let me guess," Mom said. "You're having the *best* time of your life, and you're *so* glad that I did what I did because you're happier and less worried about frivolous things."

"I might be getting there," I said, "a little." The truth is I'm not sure how I feel about it, but I have to show Mom that I'm learning.

It was kind of nice to be able to eat falafel for lunch. You couldn't have paid me to bring falafel to my last school. It was too . . . different. I would have died if people had stared at me eating. When Hunter found out that it's my favorite food he made fun of the *word*. I'm not even sure he knows what it is. Yeah, there was no way. Even though it's delicious and Hunter would have loved it if I could've persuaded him to try it.

Eva had every part of her falafel kemaj separated on her

plate—the falafel balls, the pita, the cucumbers, the potatoes—even the sauce. Mine was all tucked into my pita like it should be.

"Okay," Mom said, "so you feel deep inside your heart that this is a productive road—and you love your mother for making you do it?"

I paused to squish up my face. "I wouldn't go *that* far," I said.

Mom sighed. "Has it been terrible?" She sat down next to me. She really wanted me to succeed. She's pretty fantastic that way, even though she isn't fantastic insisting I go to a virtual school and look like the most boring person in the universe.

"It's a bit of a mess," I said. "But I can figure it out." I sounded much more confident than I felt. Hunter still didn't know who I was, and with Daebak, things were complicated.

One bright spot had been playing *The Furriest* with Keiko. She just stood there at first, completely and obviously hating being a fluffy chicken ball—a very gruff tuft of feathers with big eyes and a beak popping out from her face.

And she was scowling worse than Hunter had when he first played. But then she started saying how much she hated it, and her words came out in that helium voice. And she was a chicken.

And she laughed. It was just a little at first. But then we laughed too, and she laughed more.

And the more she talked, the more we laughed. And the more she laughed when we talked. I think it was probably the most Keiko had laughed in a while.

But I didn't know if we'd be able to persuade her to do that again.

Well, maybe.

"Eva, I saw that," Mom said.

"But . . . but . . . but," Eva stuttered. "I don't *like* the green ones."

"The 'green ones' are called cucumbers," Mom said, pointing at the ground calmly. "And even if you don't like them, that doesn't mean that you can throw them on the floor for Keniv. Pick them up and go put them in the garbage. And then eat the ones you have left."

Eva looked at the ground below her chair, huffed, then slid down until her feet touched the floor.

"Did you ever figure out why Hunter's there?" Mom asked, looking at Eva and rolling her eyes. I still think she was disappointed he was there, like she thought I could succeed more if none of my old friend group were there to influence me.

"Maybe his *really intense mom* is forcing him."

My mom nodded. "If so, she's probably a brilliant woman, and he should thank heaven that he has her in his life." She popped a tomato in her mouth. "Moms are pretty much the best. She's probably a genius."

I eye-rolled so hard I think I strained something.

"But does he know who you are?" she asked.

I shook my head.

"Nom. Nom," Eva said as she ate. Then she picked up a falafel ball and squished it between her hands.

"Eva, don't," Mom said, walking over to take the ball away and wipe Eva's fingers with a napkin.

"There's a virtual dance coming up," I said, seizing my chance to change the subject.

"Great!" Mom said. "How do you feel about that?"

"I'm not sure," I said. That was the truth. As Vanya, I can't say I was excited. Everyone else would be looking their best, and then there would be me. It wasn't like there would be a line of boys hoping to dance with me. I'd be lucky to get attention from a few friends. Hunter had asked me at the last dance, but there was no way he would ask me now. And I didn't want him to.

And then there was Daebak. He was ecstatic about the dance, probably looking forward to it more than anyone I knew. With his look and his dancing, it was like he'd been planning this the whole semester. But now I pictured him differently.

I knew who he really was.

I found him in the yearbook—Bradley Horvath. He was a big quiet kid in Mr. Richardson's class, the one everyone said peed his pants in some assembly. But I can't even imagine him as Daebak. They seem totally different.

Then again, he thinks I'm totally different from Edelle.

And he likes my virtual version better.

It all has me confused. I'm not sure what I'm feeling about it all.

"There's got to be a way to make it fun," Mom said. "If you can forget yourself and all the pressure of looking perfect in front of everyone, and just dance with your friends, dances can be such a great time."

I slowed my chewing.

"What? What did I say?" Mom asked.

I shook my head, but there was something about what she'd said that stuck with me.

"Done!" Eva said, and started getting herself out of her booster seat.

As Mom helped her, I was still thinking.

"You just gave me an amazing idea," I told Mom. I stood up and started pacing by the table. "But it would be kind of a big deal. And I don't know if the school could do it, but it would be amazing if they could." I think my pulse doubled just thinking about it. There was no way I could make it happen by myself. I'd need both the administration and the computer people on board.

"What are you talking about?" Mom asked.

"If I needed it—and it would be awesome—could you send a bunch of emails to the school?" I asked. I needed her to go all mama bear for me. I could send emails too, but Mom's help was probably the only way this would ever happen.

"I guess," Mom said. "If it's really a good idea."

I smiled. "It's a *great* idea."

CHAPTER 34

HELLO?

Hunter

I ran across the top of a wall in the obstacle course, but had to jump to keep rotating bars from knocking me off.

I leapt again.

And again.

Then I had to weave through some other barriers, then duck.

I had to be better.

Faster.

We were still going to compete together as JaVaHuDa, but if we were going to get anywhere, I was going to have to be my best. The Killer Monkeys were probably on the better side of the other teams I'd watched, but there were even a couple teams that seemed stronger than the Monkeys. And the tournament starts next week.

And I still need this.

Jasper had talked to me to smooth everything over after the whole Vanya incident. I still couldn't believe she freaked out so much. She obviously wasn't doing as well as she could. But I never would have guessed she'd claim to be Edelle. That was desperate. Plus, it turned out Jasper was right; we couldn't switch team members. We could only sign on an additional player if someone on our team couldn't play, and the extra person had to be someone totally new to the game. I looked it up. And if someone hadn't signed up yet, they probably weren't any good.

We'd increased our training over the last couple of weeks. It was a little awkward at practice and in science class, but we were starting to get along okay. I had to apologize for trying to kick Vanya off the team, and Vanya apologized for claiming to be Edelle. In some ways she was improving at the games, but in others, she was practicing distracted. She said she had a big idea she was working on, but she wouldn't really say any more. It bothered me that she wasn't more focused, especially with the tournament so close. But she was on the team, and I had to make the most of it.

So I asked Jasper if he'd work with me a little extra. He's a machine, and together we've really pushed each other. We might be able to make the difference. We were even practicing today, even though the dance was going to start in a couple of hours.

Sometimes it takes optimal dedication to get optimal results.

I ran up a ramp, then had to climb up a pole. Climbing took a little getting used to. I had to pretend my arms could wrap around the pole, and keep moving them as fast as I could up it. For just arm movement, it was surprisingly good exercise.

But Jasper hadn't shown up yet.

I finished the course with a rope swing. I swayed back and

forth—the trick is timing my jump just right to grab the rope and swing over. But I had practiced enough to figure it out.

I paused for just a minute when I was done.

Me:

Jasper, where are you?

Then I was back at it.

After I'd run through the obstacle course again, and Jasper still hadn't shown, I texted a follow-up.

Then I ran through again, trying to improve my time. The pole climb seemed like the best place I could improve. If I could get more of a jump coming in, I might be able to shave off a second or two.

Still no Jasper. Where *was* he?

I lifted up my goggles, dialed his number, then put the goggles back on. I wanted to be able to see him if he showed up at the course.

"Hello?" a woman's voice answered.

That took me by surprise. "Oh, um, sorry. I thought this was Jasper's phone," I said.

"It is," the woman answered. "I'm his mother."

"Oh," I said, "I'm his friend Hunter from school. He was going to meet me at the obstacle course to practice, but he isn't here. I was just checking up on him."

"Hunter," she said. "You're the lacrosse player. He talked about you a lot." That made me feel good. Maybe at dinner he talked about how we were totally going to rock this tournament. She sighed a little. "He really wanted that trophy."

Yeah, that was Jasper. I wanted to win, and Jasper did too, but what he really wanted was that trophy. Don't get me wrong, I like trophies too, but he's kind of obsessed.

This time we would get it. That's why we were working hard.

Wait. Did his mom just say "he *wanted* that trophy"? Like past tense? I could 100 percent guarantee that he wants it, present tense.

"Can I talk to him?" I asked.

"Unfortunately, not right now," she said. "He really isn't feeling well."

"Oh, okay," I said. "That's not good. He doesn't have the pandemic stuff, does he?"

"Nah," she said, "this is something he's faced for a long time. We're usually pretty open about it, so he may have told you. He has cystic fibrosis." He hadn't told me. I had no idea what that meant, but I didn't like the sound of it. "You might have heard him cough. He coughs a lot at the end of your practices, but he usually turns off his mic," she explained. "And it's why he's in virtual school—to make sure he's safe and has limited exposure to the virus." She let out a big breath. "But unfortunately, his lungs aren't cooperating right now. We're at the hospital."

"The hospital?" I blurted out. "Is he okay?" It was like when you suddenly noticed a member of your team on the field, reeling with an injury, and you have no idea what was wrong. No—this was worse than that. There was always the chance a teammate just got the wind knocked out of them and would be fine in a few minutes. If Jasper was already in the hospital, this was really serious.

"He should be fine," his mother said. "He's had to do this before. The doctors have him on some different medicines, and he's responding well. They're going to keep an eye on him for a few days."

Relief poured over me. "Oh, that's good," I said. "So he's going to be okay?" She had just said that he was, but I still wanted to make sure.

"Yes," she said. I hadn't realized that I had been flexing, but I noticed when I released the tension. "Thanks so much for teaming up with him. He's loved it. Something like this happened to him last year during soccer, and he wasn't able to play the last part of the season." She paused. "He doesn't think it's fair to have your body kick you off a team. You know? He thinks if he'd been able to play, they would have won a trophy." She paused again and sniffled a little. "And now it's happening again. I hope real hard you all can find someone to replace him."

"What?" I said. "What do you mean? He's definitely still on the team. We don't want to replace him." We couldn't, not at this point of the competition. And really not at all. No one played like he did. He was the one who brought us all together. And as much as it bothered me sometimes, he was also our coach—he really helped us all. Going without him was like having one of your money players on the injured list and replacing them with someone who hadn't played before. "He's not going to be okay by the time the tournament starts?"

"He's doing well already," his mom said, "but the doctors won't let him do that much activity for the next few weeks. His lungs have to recover. He's going to have to sit it out." She let out another tired sigh. "He's heartbroken." Her voice cracked a little. "Again." Her voice quivered. I couldn't imagine lying in a hospital bed instead of competing, two years in a row. "But," she said, sniffling a little, but her voice growing brighter, "I told him that if you guys are willing, we'd love to have you over to see him when he gets home. You'd have to wear masks and meet distanced outside, but he could *really* use something to look forward to." The way she said *really* hit me. She couldn't give him the tournament, so she was trying to give him some sort of substitution. It wouldn't be nearly as cool, but she was trying.

"Of course. Absolutely," I said, my mind going numb, "but there really isn't any way that he can recover in time?"

"I'm sorry," she said. "He has to follow his doctor's orders, or he might get sicker. I'll tell him that you called," she said. "Goodbye."

I hung up, and immediately wanted to punch something. I wanted to barrel through a wall. I wanted to run and not stop.

Jasper was sick. He had put together a team, and we'd practiced and practiced and practiced. We'd worked so hard. And he kept us together because he thought we could win. But he wasn't going to be able to make it.

And without Jasper, there was absolutely no way to win this tournament.

CHAPTER 35

TWO DANCES

Hunter

My fists beat against my chest.

Doot. Doot. Doot. Doot. Doot. Doot. Doot. Doot.

The drop hit the same time as both my fists against my chest.

Heart.

I flexed.

I touched my head.

Mind.

I was going to make the absolute most of this. I had to. I just had the tournament ripped out from under me. Without Jasper, we didn't have a chance. We couldn't replace a guy like that with leftovers who hadn't signed up.

And that meant that me, Daebak, and Vanya were done. It was time to bow out. And I was going to have to tell them.

I had three bald spots, and I'd just lost the thing I wanted most in this weird school.

I hit my chest again. I had to focus. This was like the worst possible situation, but at least I had the dance. Me and two of the prettiest girls in the school were about to meet up. I could still have a good time and then figure out what to do next.

A few moments later, I was walking next to Grace and Ruby.

"I'm so excited," Grace said, dancing a little to the beat we could hear in the halls. It was thumping loud. I couldn't feel it in my feet like I could with a real dance, but it echoed pretty well in my ears.

"Me too," Ruby said. She wasn't dancing, more like bouncing, like a really excited walk. They both looked great in their new virtual dresses. The school had approved one more outfit for everyone, so I was wearing a pink button-up with jeans.

"Let's do this," I said. My whole world felt like it was falling out from under me, but I was still going to try to dance on top of it. I didn't know how to fix it, but if there was a way, I'd find it.

Or maybe I'd find Edelle. There couldn't be a better time. I had texted that I'd love to meet her at the dance, but she hadn't texted back. I still don't know why she's hiding from me.

Unless Grace is actually Edelle. If so, I didn't know why she wouldn't answer any of my questions, but that might be kind of epic. Then she would have been friends with me the whole time. And with the tournament gone, it would just be great to know I was hanging out with her.

I still couldn't believe that Vanya had claimed to be her. There was no way.

And it was because of Vanya that there were two rooms we could choose from for the dance tonight. When I logged on for the dance, NovaMillennium lady had another announcement waiting for me. She explained that one room would be the dance that NovaMillennium had planned. It would be held in the varsity gym, but Vanya had approached them with another idea that some of the programmers really liked. NovaMillennium lady seemed pretty excited about it, but she wouldn't tell us any more about it. It would be in the small gym.

I guess that was what Vanya had been working on. But to me, it sounded like the varsity gym was for the big time and the small gym for all the others. I'd stick with varsity. I definitely didn't trust Vanya's version of fun.

Grace and Ruby wanted to be a few minutes late, and I agreed. That way we can make an entrance. If you're the first one there, there's no one else to react to. And I definitely needed the distraction.

In the open gym doors ahead I could get a peek at the dance: a few people moving and swaying, colorful decorative paper streamed from the walls and even on the basketball hoop. The crowd was really thin along the edge I could see, but that was normal. It's out in the middle where the real fun would be. We'd see the core of the party after we stepped in. And I was a core-of-the-party kind of guy.

With every step we could feel the pulse of the music more and more, and both Grace and Ruby moved to it.

We walked in.

"Oh, yeah," I yelled, and clapped my hands. It felt a little hollow, but I wasn't giving up.

Grace stopped completely, looking at me. And then Ruby looked at both of us.

There were only thirty or forty people in the room.

What was going on?

It was like showing up to a game, and the other team had forfeited. Or maybe we'd forfeited. There was no chance to play. No energy. No excited fans.

Maybe it was worse than that—like a zombie apocalypse had hit, and there just weren't enough kids left to still have a dance.

A girl and a boy passed us, walking together. "Let's go back to the other room," the boy said.

"*Definitely*," she said.

We saw a group of three girls leave as well, headed toward the small gym. Apparently, even those who'd survived the apocalypse were leaving.

Whatever reason this dance wasn't going well was because of whatever was happening in the other room. Vanya's room.

Had she really had a good idea? It better not be making us waltz or square dance or something. That sounded like something she'd come up with. But that couldn't be right—that definitely wouldn't have won over the crowd. They wouldn't be leaving this dance for something like that. Or maybe I'd really underestimated her. Maybe she had some really good ideas that I just didn't get.

"This dance is pretty dead," Ruby said. "Let's check the other room."

Grace and I agreed and we were off. We might as well at least see what was going on.

As we approached, the doors were closed. But we could hear music pounding and all sorts of laughter. It sounded like a total party.

"Now this sounds right," Ruby said, starting to dance-walk again.

Across the door was a sign saying, "You've never gone to a dance like this."

I opened the doors.

My heart took a cheap shot, totally blindsided.

I came ready. I'd worked my game-day ritual. I had needed this.

But not *this*.

"What's going on here?" Grace asked. "And what's wrong with my voice?"

Ruby laughed. "No way. This is crazy."

And I looked down. Somehow Vanya had done it. She got NovaMillennium and the school administrators on board. I was no longer me. I was the fluffiest, roundest bunny in the universe, in a room of fluffy animals dancing and laughing like crazy.

This was the furriest dance in existence. My world had been crumbling, and this just blasted it into smaller pieces. It felt like one more terrible thing that I just couldn't take.

CHAPTER 36

REMEMBER THIS

Edelsabeth

"What do you think, Keiko?" I asked in my high-pitched voice. "No one can worry about how they look here." I was moving from side to side to the beat.

"Nope," she said, not dancing at all, her name in fluffy letters in front of her. I asked if that feature could be turned off, so everyone could be undercover, but in the end, it was too difficult. And it did make it easier to find your friends. It would be total confusion without it.

But if you'd ever heard a puffball chicken say "nope" in a high-pitched voice with almost no emotion, it might instantly make your night better.

"Come on," Daebak said in his cute voice, inviting her to dance, moving like there was no tomorrow. That fuzzy pink gerbil ball had all the moves.

Keiko watched for a moment. "Nope."

I think part of Daebak was a little disappointed about this

dance. He'd probably be living his dream if he was spending the whole time in the other dance room. With his pink hair, outfit, and moves, it was like he'd been waiting for this the entire school year. So I promised him that we would all go in for the second hour of the dance. And I promised him the best video yet.

"What about this?" he asked, and whirled around, then did a quick step back.

I raised a furry thumb.

We came up with the idea of splicing together footage of him doing some of the same moves as a gerbil and then as his avatar at the other dance. It would be totally unique and probably get him the most views yet.

I still couldn't picture him as Bradley Horvath. Daebak is so happy and excited. Bradley never seemed that way at all. He always seemed to want to be alone, so everyone left him alone. I never would have guessed he'd want someone to film him dancing.

"Keiko," Daebak said, dancing next to her, "I'll teach you some moves. Please, please be in this video with me."

"No," she said. She joined in a lot faster in *The Furriest* than she did here. I guess she was prepared for the cute craziness and was resisting it a little now.

"You know you want to," Daebak prodded.

This whole thing had turned out better than I thought it would. I sent a video to the administration telling them about my experience at the school, about Keiko and what she'd said about dances, and then pitched my idea. I even found blogs about what tweens worry about at dances and sent them too. My mother sent emails as well.

At first they responded that they would think about it, and I didn't think I would hear any more since the dance was so close. I'm pretty sure Mom wrote another email. She can be pretty intense.

And then they wrote me back saying that normally they wouldn't do this kind of thing, but one of their designers thought it was a great idea, and that it wouldn't take that much work to mesh the code for *The Furriest* with the dance. But then they reported he'd worked through the night to make it happen today.

And now the room was *tons* more popular than the regular dance. People were totally letting go and having a blast. It was working—proof that sometimes we just want to forget about how we look and have fun.

Except Keiko. At least so far.

"Where's Jasper?" I asked. Daebak was great, but I think Keiko might have danced if Jasper was here. She seemed to have a little bit of a soft spot for him.

"I've texted him, but no answer," Daebak said. "He probably practiced too long with Hunter and is just running late."

That made sense.

"Okay," Daebak said to Keiko, "if you won't do *my* dance, just do that thing you did when you made fun of everyone else trying to look cool."

"Ugh," she said, but it came out super squeaky, and made her laugh just a little.

Daebak tried to remember it, stepping back and moving his arms crazy.

"You're making it worse," Keiko said.

He did it even bigger.

She groaned again, then unexpectedly launched into it, moving her arms like spaghetti noodles, and shifting her body in weird directions.

"So awesome," Daebak said, high-pitched, and tried to match her movements.

I don't think it was quite what Daebak had in mind for his video, but it was hilarious. And awesome.

I wouldn't record unless I had Keiko's permission, and I didn't think she was ready for that. But I wanted to remember this. For at least a few moments, we just forgot about all the pressure and had fun.

"That would make an amazing video," I said. Keiko immediately stopped.

"Ugh," she said.

And it came out all adorable. And Keiko couldn't help but laugh about it again.

CHAPTER 37

DISCOVERY

Hunter

I searched the gym full of annoying puffballs for Vanya.

She'd ruined it. I was trying to dance while everything was falling out from under me, and she'd made it absolutely stupid. I needed to forget about the tournament, forget about the bald spots, forget that one of my best friends in this place was stuck in a hospital room instead of here. And then the dance was like this.

Plus, I had to tell her and Daebak the bad news. Maybe part of me even wanted to.

I had told Grace and Ruby that I'd be back in a minute.

"Hey," I said when I found the weird mouse and gerbil, looking puffy and idiotic. I recognized their ridiculous round avatars from when we played *The Furriest* together. When they turned around, yep, there were their names in fuzzy letters in front of them. Vanya and Daebak. They were dancing with a puffy chicken named Keiko as well. And for some reason, that reminded me a little of Jasper's duck and made me angrier. And it made me angry that any puffy animal ball would remind me of him. He's more than that. He's a competitor. A friend. A teammate. He's awesome, not completely ridiculous.

Plus, Jasper had been excited to come to the dance. He should be at the dance in the other gym with me and our friends, not in some hospital room.

"Vanya," I said, and was instantly ticked about how high-pitched my voice was, "why did you do this?"

Vanya looked over. "Why did I do what?"

"You're ruining the dance," I said, the whole room full of bouncing crazy fuzzy animals just irritating me more. They were all giggling and laughing like crazy little people. This wasn't for junior high. This was for kindergarten. How could anyone think this was a good idea?

Daebak stepped in. "Hey, calm down. She's not ruining anything." He tried to be all tough, but no one can be tough looking like a puffball. "If you don't like it, go to the other gym."

I had just had enough. I pushed him out of the way.

But he was a perfectly round gerbil and he rolled like in the game, tumbling several feet like a bowling ball. He stopped just before he would have knocked into another group of animals dancing.

So far, that had been the only good part of tonight.

"Stop it," Vanya said.

But I kept talking, calling out loud enough over the music. "Did you hear that Jasper is sick?" My anger rose. Something about saying it out loud made it more real.

"What? No," she said.

"What's wrong?" the chicken next to her said. I didn't want to talk to her. I didn't even know who she was.

"He's in the hospital," I said. Vanya moved her little hands over her mouth. "His mom says he'll be okay, but he isn't going to be able to play in the tournament."

"That's terrible," Daebak said. He had been walking back at me all angry, but he heard my news.

"I wouldn't make anything like that up," I said. Some people had started watching us. Probably because of the shouting. Oh, and making Daebak look like a bowling ball. But I really didn't care. "So that means we're out. We can't win without him."

"We could still play," Daebak started. "He would want us to. Maybe we could find someone else—"

I didn't *want* to replace him. Not for anybody else. He was our team captain, the one who got us all together. It was his team. The thought boiled me more inside.

And even if we did try to replace him, we had absolutely no chance, especially with Vanya still making mistakes.

I hated this. All of it.

I pushed Daebak again—this time he flew off the ground several feet and then rolled, crashing into about five animals. Again, it looked a little like *The Furriest* game. It was programmed for the animals to be able to boost each other up and to roll. I guess I boosted him in a totally different way. In a *quit-saying-dumb-things* kind of way.

It felt oddly satisfying.

More people turned and looked at us. I didn't care.

"Stop that," Vanya said, and ran to help Daebak up. A few

moments later, they were right back. "We'll talk to Jasper and make sure. Maybe there's a mistake."

"There's no mistake," I said. "He's in the hospital." Just thinking about him again made me furious. And the fact that I wasn't at a real dance, and I was standing here as the stupidest fluffy bunny in the universe made it all so much worse. I couldn't even be me. Not here. Not in regular classes. Not in the tournament. Nowhere. I couldn't focus. I couldn't stand out. I couldn't achieve anything.

"There has to be something we can do for—" Daebak started. But I'd had it.

I picked him up. In real life, my gloves felt a little resistance, but in general he didn't weigh a thing. I threw him to the side like a boost again. He flew through the air, hit the bleachers, and rolled right back to me.

Again, oddly satisfying.

"Stop it," Vanya yelled.

But I wasn't done. I picked him up one more time and had a better idea. I would do what you do with round things on a basketball court. I walked a few feet to the end of the court, and then I heaved him upward, shooting him like a basketball.

I don't know if I've ever loved a basketball shot more. Seriously, watching a fluffy gerbil roll around the rim and then stop halfway into the basket was sheer beauty.

And what was better was—he was totally stuck. With those little tiny arms and legs, I don't think he could get himself out.

The whole place erupted in laughter.

Vanya's eyes got huge, "Hunter Athanasopoulos!" she yelled.

"You don't care about anything unless it's about *you*. About making *you* look good. About what *you* want."

Maybe I should shoot her in a basket too. It would serve her right to be stuck up there with her little friend. But both of them wouldn't fit, and she wasn't worth it. I felt my anger fading into emptiness and turned to leave.

"You and I danced twice at the dance last year," Vanya said.

"What?" I said turning back. That didn't make any sense at all.

"I was wearing a blue dress," she said.

"What are you talking about?"

"We used to go to get shakes together," she said. "You got cookie dough, I got mint chocolate chip, and I dipped my fries in it. And you think it's gross."

I *did* get cookie dough shakes, and fries in shakes *are* gross. But why was she saying all of this? How did she know?

"You and Fetu have a handshake, and you do it every time you meet." She was talking louder. "I was there watching both of you when you won the lacrosse tournament. Me and Kennedy."

My stomach started to lurch.

"You've been texting me, trying to find me in this school."

My insides hardened now, feeling heavy.

"You texted me asking if we could go to this dance."

I shook my head. "You're faking. You found out information."

"I have a dog named Keniv and a little sister named Eva," she kept talking. "You have an older brother named Ryker. And," she said, shifting a little, "if I'm really her, you'll get a text from her right . . ." She paused for a second. "Now."

I felt my pocket buzz. I pulled off my goggles to check it out.

It was from Edelle.

Two words: *It's me.*

"I've been right in front of you the whole time, but because I didn't *look* like me, you ignored me. You looked right past me. You texted through our conversations. You only talked with me to see if I could help you. You passed me over for prettier girls. You tried to kick me off the team." She stepped closer to me. "You just yelled at me, telling me that all of this," she gestured around her, "was a terrible idea. You've humiliated Daebak, who's a way better friend than you were." She paused. "I'm not sure we ever were really friends."

CHAPTER 38

OUT

Bradley

Stuck in a basketball hoop, the whole school watching.

My name in furry letters for everyone to read.

It's amazing how you can hear every laugh of hundreds when they're all laughing at you.

All sorts of cameras came out to take pictures.

I was supposed to be making the most epic video yet.

Nope—the total and complete opposite. I was the star of dozens of horrible, awful, embarrassing ones, ones probably already winging their way to the school's MeetUp, not to mention YouTube and TikTok.

I was supposed to be having the time of my life with my friends, but now I was flapping my little hands and feet, trying to shift my weight, trying to rock myself out of the hoop.

But I was totally and completely stuck.

More laughs.

I tried again.

More pictures and video.

I'd known I was going to be famous after tonight; I just had the reason totally wrong.

And then the laughs died down as Vanya started yelling at Hunter. And I heard what she said. Every word.

I clicked out of the system. I went from completely humiliated, stuck in a basketball hoop, to gone. From a nightmare to back home in my pajama pants.

From Daebak back to Bradley.

It was the fastest, best escape anywhere.

But it was like I'd fallen right back to where I used to be, standing with wet pants in the third grade assembly, totally humiliated in front of the whole school.

It was the sequel to my nightmare.

Daebak was dead.

I had tried to be a new me and this is what happened.

I just couldn't escape it. I thought I could, but I couldn't.

It was part of me, something inside of me. It didn't matter how hard I tried, it just always ended the same.

I flung off all the VR equipment.

I turned off my phone. I turned off my lights, and fell on my bed.

I was lying there awake trying to forget everything when my parents peeked in. They whispered my name, but I didn't answer. I didn't want to be conscious.

In my mind, I could still hear them all laughing.

CHAPTER 39

SPRINT

Hunter

I slammed down my goggles, dropped my controllers, and ran out of my house.

And I sprinted up the street.

It didn't matter that I'd already gone for a run this morning, or that I wasn't wearing my exercise gear, or that my mom called after me. I just had to go.

And I ran.

I didn't worry about warming up or pacing myself. I just pounded my legs one after the other, pushing myself over the pavement.

Edelle was Vanya this whole time. Why? Why didn't she tell me?

Step. Step. Step.

Step. Step. Step.

My legs started aching quicker than normal, but my brain ached a million times worse. So I pushed harder and harder.

Why would she do that? How was I supposed to know it was her? There was no way.

It didn't make any sense. I felt like I'd been set up. Like there was a trap set, and there was no way I could have avoided it.

I pushed my feet faster as I came up on a hill.

Good. That would really burn. I wanted the burn.

I had asked her to help me find Edelle. I tried to keep Jasper from inviting her to join our team, and then I tried to kick her off. I ruined her dance. I wouldn't have, if I had known. Why would she look like that? She was beautiful. Why not be herself? There was no way I could have known.

And then I embarrassed her friend in front of everyone.

I should have been her friend.

I pushed my legs harder.

She didn't even act the same way, right? I searched my mind for ways she was different.

A blue sedan passed me, then pulled over a few houses ahead of me. I knew that sedan. Ryker was inside. He must have heard me leave.

I turned around, running back the way I came, picking up the pace. I didn't want to see him.

I heard the door shut and heard steps.

I ran faster, turning down a side road. I didn't want anyone with me.

Edelle had given me a test I couldn't pass and then looked at me like she was all ashamed that I hadn't. Like I was a total jerk.

More steps from my brother behind me.

I ran faster. I could beat him, and I was going to prove it. I could feel the sweat running down the sides of my face, and I didn't care.

Plus, I was going bald. I didn't even know if my hat was covering all my bald spots right now. I'd lost Edelle already, but once Kennedy knew, I'd lose her too. Even Fetu would probably think I was a freak. That is if I hadn't lost them already. They weren't responding much lately; probably too busy with their regular school and new friends.

I pushed hard for another block, and then something in me started to give. I slowed a little.

Footsteps.

I hated this. I knew what he would say. It made me want to run more, so I did, but then I slowed again, this time even more.

Soon he was running next to me.

I looked over at him, brushing my face with my hand. I couldn't tell anymore what was sweat and what was tears.

But he didn't say anything. He just nodded.

And then we kept running.

He slowed when I did, and sped up to match me. We ran twice as far as normal, until I just couldn't go anymore.

And then we started to walk. I didn't want to. I wanted to run. I didn't want him to be able to catch his breath to speak. But I didn't have any energy left.

He didn't say anything. I looked over and he just nodded again, walking slowly next to me.

My face was still wet, but I knew it was tears. My sweat was calming down, and I could feel the breeze against it.

"Aren't you going to say anything?" I practically screamed.

He shrugged. "I don't have anything to say," he said. "I don't even know what's going on."

And I walked some more. And he walked with me.

We were still about a half mile away from my house when I told him everything.

CHAPTER 40

FAKE

Bradley

I faked my way through breakfast. I did my best impression of Bradley on a normal day. Of course, my parents asked about the dance, and I even plastered on a smile and told them a lot of the good things that had happened. About Vanya's idea, and my friends, and laughing. It reminded me of the last few years of school when my parents would ask about my day, and I had told them the littlest shred of something good that had happened and then pretended like the terrible didn't exist. I wore a lot of fake smiles then too.

But after my parents went to work, I climbed back into bed. We obviously weren't having team practice before school—there was no team anymore. And I wouldn't go if there was.

I slept through the start of class. When I woke I just lay there, not really focusing on anything.

I didn't get on my phone or Netflix. Or my VR. And I didn't leave my room.

I just tried not to think. Tried not to relive everything. Or imagine the next bunch of whispers I'd hear in the hallway or in class or the commons.

I didn't care how many periods I missed.

Then someone knocked on my door.

Not the apartment door, but my bedroom door. Which to be honest, kind of freaked me out.

"Hey, buddy, can I come in?"

Dad.

I didn't say anything. I just kept staring at the wall.

"Say yes," he said, "because I'm coming in and I'd rather do it with your permission than not."

I exhaled long and loud. "Yes," I said.

He stepped in. He was still wearing his mask and his work apron.

"Dad, you can't be here," I said. "You don't have enough workers for everything." He had been working a ton of hours lately. Several of his employees had gotten sick, or had people in their family that had gotten sick, and there weren't enough people to cover for them. So my dad worked for them.

He nodded. "True, but your mom works twenty minutes further away, and we've been getting texts that our son hasn't logged on to school."

I should have guessed that would happen.

"You could just text," I said.

"Oh, I did," he said, and reached over and grabbed my phone. "I texted about twenty times." He moved his finger across my phone's screen, but nothing happened. "But it looks like this isn't on."

Right. I had turned it off last night after everything happened.

He turned on my phone and sat down while it loaded. I guess he wanted to make sure he could still get in touch later on. "What's going on?" he asked.

"Dad, you're under lots of pressure. You've got to get back to work," I said.

He nodded. "And apparently you're under a lot of pressure too. So this is my most important work right now." He just sat there, not moving. I wanted him to leave so bad, but then I also didn't want him to move. I was half and half, an emotional minotaur again.

We sat there in silence for a while.

And then I told him how everything had gone terribly wrong.

"I'm not sure I understand all this," he said. "How the avatars work and everything." I wasn't surprised by that. "But I understand that your situation stinks. And I'm sorry." He paused. "And," he said, "I'm also really proud of you."

"What?" I said.

"I'm proud of you for trying. Trying to dance. Trying to make friends. Trying out the games. Trying to stand up for what you think is right. That's hard."

It was a nice idea, but I shook my head. "I'm not doing that again," I said.

"You have to," he said. "You have to show up and try. Sometimes it will work, and sometimes it won't—but that's how you really live." He shifted a little. "You have a lot to offer, Bradley. But it's only when you try that you'll know how much."

Maybe he was right, maybe he was wrong, but I didn't have the energy to argue with him. "Thanks," I said, hoping that would stop the you-can-do-it lecture.

"And I know something else," Dad said. "You've got some good friends."

He looked down at my phone. He seemed to scan it for a while. "Good friends," he repeated. "It looks like you've missed about eighty-seven messages."

"Eighty-seven?"

"Yeah," my dad said. "Now, I'm sure twenty or thirty of them are from me and your mom, but something tells me some other people are trying to reach you."

I didn't know what to say.

"Looks to me like people appreciate how hard you're trying. Better not quit now." He set my phone on my desk. "You don't have to go to school today," he said, "but you may want to text your friends back."

Again, another quote I don't think anyone else has ever heard from their dad.

CHAPTER 41

MESSAGES

Bradley

Vanya: Yesterday 7:44 pm

Daebak, I'm so sorry that happened. That was not cool.

Vanya: Yesterday 7:51 pm

Are you okay? Do you want to talk?

Vanya: Yesterday 7:53 pm

I'm sorry. I should have told you who I really was. I'm sorry about all of this.

Vanya: Yesterday 7:57 pm

Seriously, are you okay?

Keiko: Yesterday 8:05 pm

Vanya gave me ur number. I just want you to know that I'm going to terrorize Hunter in your honor. You say the word and I'll do it.

Vanya: Yesterday 8:07 pm

Wanna talk? Are you mad at me?

Keiko: Yesterday 8:09 pm

Here are my ideas for revenge:

Spam his social media with pictures of angry goats, like thousands of them.

Find his address and send him a donut in the mail, but instead of cream inside, there are Carolina reapers—the hottest peppers in the world.

Or catfood.

Or dirt.

Or all three of them.

Or Oreos filled with glue.

Jasper: Yesterday 8:15 pm

Sorry I wasn't there. I think you heard that I wasn't feeling good.

Vanya told me what happened tonight. Are you ok?

And don't worry about me. I'm doing fine.

Vanya: Yesterday 8:16 pm

Call me.

Keiko: Yesterday 8:18 pm

We talk to the administration and have them make Hunter sit inside a basketball hoop for the rest of the semester.

Or he has to attend the rest of the year as a fluffy animal.

Or we find real wild animals and let them loose in his house.

Vanya: Yesterday 8:21 pm

Keiko: Yesterday 8:26 pm

We could put on the internet that we're having a contest to see who can sound the most like an angry pig and have people call his phone number.

We give him a whole bunch of gift cards and one of them has ten cents just to give him hope. The rest have absolutely no money on them.

Vanya: Yesterday 9:34 pm

Good night. Just know that I still want to be your friend. I hope you do too.

Vanya: Today 8:23 am

I've been looking for you this morning. Again, I hope you're okay.

Jasper: Today 8:25 am

Just checking in buddy. I didn't hear from you last night.

Keiko: Today 8:27 am

You know that practical joke where you fill someone's toilet with jello so it firms up? I wonder if we could do that to his whole house.

Vanya: Today 8:31 am

Where are you? Science started already.

Hunter got suspended for the day so he's not here. And of course Jasper's gone too. It's just me at our table.

Maybe just log in for science class? Daebak?

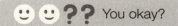 You okay?

Keiko: Today 9:15 am

We could put life-sized cardboard cutouts of angry clowns in his shower.

Vanya: Today 9:20 am

What's your address? I'm coming over at lunch or after school.

Keiko: Today 9:45 am

We could put paint on the inside of his goggles, so when he takes them off he has paint around his eyes like he's a raccoon.

Vanya: Today 9:50 am

Seriously, what's your address?

Keiko: Today 10:17 am

We could fill his room with water balloons.

Or fire ants.

Or water balloons covered in fire ants.

Vanya: Today 10:20 am

I'll find your address if you don't give it to me.

Jasper: Today 10:37 am

??? Still haven't heard from you Daebak. Maybe I should start spamming you with memes until you answer.

Vanya: Today 10:59 am

I found it. I'm coming over.

CHAPTER 42

DON'T COME OVER

Bradley

Me: 11:02 am

> Don't come over.

And I waited.

No response.

But there was no way she knew where to find me. It wasn't like my address was listed anywhere.

I jumped up and looked down at my unmatched socks, dancing panda pajamas, and Bubble Girls T-shirt. That's a terrible combination. And if Vanya was coming over, I at least had to change. And what about the apartment? We weren't messy people, but what if Mom had been folding my underwear in the living room?

I peeked my head outside my door.

Safe on the underwear.

Wait. No. (Still no underwear, just had another thought.)

Not Vanya. Edelle.

It wouldn't be my best friend from virtual school. It would be the popular girl that all the boys love on some list I didn't care about. The girl that ignored me. The one that laughed at me. The one that requested another partner in history class. The one that sent those mean things about Marie.

Her.

Here.

I checked my phone. She hadn't responded.

But Edelle couldn't find me, right? It wasn't like she could just look me up on some virtual school roster? In fact, nothing at virtual school was under the name Bradley; it was all under Daebak.

I was safe.

Wait.

Realization hit me, my stomach dropped, and I stopped moving.

She knew.

I had told her all of those stories about me and Edelle—and if she was really Edelle, she could figure out that I was Bradley.

And there couldn't be that many Horvaths in our middle-school boundaries.

She knew.

Me: 11:10 am

> Don't come.

No answer.

I quickly jumped into some jeans and a blue collared shirt. I looked at myself in the mirror. The boring brown hair poked up in odd directions. I got it wet and matted it down. My face was so terribly far from anything Instagram-worthy. Edelle and I didn't even belong in the same room.

But even if she came, I didn't have to open the door. I didn't have to talk to her.

I checked my phone. Nothing.

My doorbell rang.

I froze.

I didn't know what to do but just stand there and pretend I hadn't heard it.

I could hear the lights buzzing.

My breath became shallow.

My heart felt like the fade-out at the end of a song.

After a few more seconds, I tiptoed over and looked through the peephole. I could only see her eyes over her mask and long dark hair.

Edelle Dahan-Miller was at my apartment.

There was no way I was going to let her in.

CHAPTER 43

CAN WE TALK?

Edelsabeth

I rang the doorbell and waited.

And then I did it again. And again. And again. I hoped I had the right apartment, because if I didn't, I was being incredibly obnoxious.

It took seven times before he finally answered. I had to prove that I wasn't going away.

Bradley Horvath looked so different from Daebak. Daebak gave off this put-together, too-cool-for-school vibe. Bradley looked like he'd been in his bed all day. He'd tried to tame some of his hair, but it was still poking up in a few places. And part of his shirt was hooked on his ribs, not pulled down all the way, like he had just put it on.

It was hard to imagine him and Daebak as the same person.

Maybe he thought the same about me and Vanya.

Bradley and I knew each other, but we didn't.

"Hey," I said, and tried to smile big. Of course, under the

mask I wasn't really sure how much good it would do. I hoped he could see it in my eyes. This couldn't be easy for him, which was clear from the *don't come* texts and not answering the door.

"Hey," he answered. No smile. "Oh, mask," he said, then reached toward the side of the door to grab a mask off a hook.

I felt so awkward. We'd never really spent time together as who we really were.

"Can we talk?" I asked.

He took a hot second, but nodded and opened the door further.

"Thanks," I said, walking into the apartment. "I was kind of terrified that you wouldn't let me in."

"I was kind of worried that I would," he said, closing the door.

I kept smiling, trying to break the tension, but there was probably a lot of truth to what he said.

His apartment was nice. He half-gestured toward the living room, so I walked in and sat on the sofa, the small grocery bag I'd brought with me swishing quietly.

"Sorry I didn't respond to your texts," he said. "I mean, besides telling you not to come over. I just . . . I had left my phone off . . . And fell asleep . . . Then I had to read the other texts first." He stopped, sighed, then sat in the chair on the other side of the room. "It's been a rough twenty-four hours."

"I'm not mad about the texts. I get it," I said. "I just couldn't stop worrying about you."

"Thanks," he said, but he raised an eyebrow.

I reached into my bag and pulled out a chocolate truffle, its green wrapper crinkling. "This is what my little sister thinks always helps when you are having a horrible day."

He reached out and took it, looked at it a moment, then smiled. "You have a smart little sister."

I shrugged. "She's three."

He set the chocolate next to him. "Still smart." I handed him the rest of the bag of truffles.

He looked away, then he said the words I knew were coming. "So . . . you really are Edelle."

I smiled, but it felt hollow. "Yeah," I said, "I'm really sorry about—"

"It's okay," he interrupted, glancing at me then looking down.

"No," I said, "I'm sorry, Bradley. I'm really, really sorry." Saying his name felt weird. I'd been calling him something completely different this whole time. But I needed to say it. It felt important to have his name spoken. I waited for that to sink in. I still hadn't completely wrapped my brain around the idea that this boy in front of me was Daebak.

"So, how long have you known?" he asked.

"A while," I said, "after you told me that story about what I did in Mr. Richardson's class. I did a little detective work and figured it out."

He groaned.

"No, I needed to know. Thank you for telling me. I've kind of felt like garbage about it, thinking about the way I ignored you, and laughed at you." My emotions caught a little.

There was a long pause, and he looked at me. He looked

down at his hands, then back at me. "You don't have to be friends with me anymore," he said.

I didn't see that coming. "What? That's not what I want, not why I came here. I don't find people's addresses and bring them chocolates if I don't want to be their friend." I spoke a little faster, hoping that somehow my words would convince him better. "I want to fix this. Hanging out with you in a weird virtual program making amazing dance videos and playing video games that I'm not even sure I like . . . it's been pretty great. Like, I've been happier than I was all last year in the top ten."

He sighed a little. "Those videos were really fun to make." And for just a second, his shoulder shifted slightly, and his head bounced to a rhythm, and I saw Daebak. "And Parker's site is stupid." Then his brows bunched together. "You really didn't like the games?"

I couldn't help but shrug. "I'm not really a gamer. I mostly just played for the company."

I could tell he smiled under his mask, then it faded. "Oh, Hunter," he said, flatly.

That wasn't what I meant, but it was kind of true. "I partially did it for him, too," I said. "But I did it for you just as much."

He sat up a little taller.

"Listen," I said, "it took me not looking like me, and you not looking like you for me to realize how amazing you are. That's weird, right? But you're really cool. You're fun and unique, and smart, and great to work with, and a great friend, and an amazing dancer." I tried to mimic his chair dance move from earlier but I'm sure it was terrible. But it made him laugh. "I had no idea all of last year that you danced. I didn't really know you at all. You were amazing and right in front of me, and I just didn't . . . see you."

I would never in a million years have guessed this is what was inside of Bradley Horvath.

"And," I said, more emotions creeping up, "because of this weird VR school—" I slowed. "I know what it feels like to be right in front of someone and have them not see me." I thought about Hunter, and him texting through our conversations, asking me if I had seen Edelle, trying to kick me off the team. "And I hated it. I hated it so bad."

And then I saw a tear well up in Bradley's eye.

I imagined what it must have been like to be him at Balderstein Middle. Just ready to make a friend, to laugh, to hang out, to be part of it all, but nobody would even take the time to see him. To know him.

I wanted to hug him, but I didn't know if he'd let me. "You're my best friend right now," I said. "Maybe that's stupid. Sorry if that's weird for you. But I can't lose you." I blinked hard. "I know you now."

"I'm not mad at you," he said. "Not really. I mean, I was, kind of. Maybe I still am a little bit. But it's okay."

"Still friends?" I asked, wiping my eye.

He nodded. "Yeah," he said, but something in his tone made it sound like he wasn't entirely convinced.

"Good, because I still owe you a video," I said, remembering the ruined dance.

His mask moved a little as he smiled underneath.

"You pick the place and time," I said. "Be Daebak or be Bradley. You decide. Both are cool."

His head tilted. I wondered if he might not have ever thought of doing a video of himself, but there was no way I was going to push him on it. Especially because I had to push him on something else.

"But," I said, "I need you to do something that you might not like." It felt strange saying it, like I was risking destroying all of this. But we had to.

"What?"

"You've got a couple of days, but we've got to go somewhere, in person."

CHAPTER 44

GAME OVER

Hunter

"I can't go," I told Ryker, who was doing push-ups in the workout corner of our basement. He had invited me to exercise, then asked me about whether or not I was going to meet up at Jasper's. Sometimes I thought he only offered to work out or run with me so he could tell me how to live my life.

Jasper had texted that he'd be out of the hospital in two days and wanted us to come visit. All of us. Together. In person.

It was a total setup.

And it would be the most awkward, terrible thing in the universe. They all knew what I'd done. I had totally missed who Edelle was, ruined her dance, and humiliated her best friend.

I was a total jerk to Edelle Dahan-Miller.

I hadn't known it was her, but I'd still done it.

I was terrible to one of my best friends, the girl that gave me huge butterflies and who I was nervous to ask to dance. The girl who came to my lacrosse games. The girl I winked at and flirted with. A girl I really wanted to impress.

And by the texts she was finally sending me, she was *ticked*.

Part of all this wasn't fair, like a trap. How was I supposed to have known it was her? She keeps texting that I should have treated her better anyway, even if I didn't know. That's the point. I should try to notice the people around me, not just the good-looking, or talented, or popular people.

I hated that she said that. I wasn't like that.

But I kept thinking about it.

I wish she would have just told me who she was in the first place. That would have stopped all of this.

Well, maybe.

I still could barely even picture Edelle as Vanya. She wasn't the same. Vanya didn't give me butterflies. And I actually wondered how I would have treated her even if I had known. I mean, I'm sure it would have been awesome at first, but after a while, I don't know.

Maybe Edelle was kind of right. And I didn't want to face her.

And Jasper seemed upset with me too. Like I wasn't being a team player. Like I could have somehow not freaked out when I found out he was sick, and the tournament I'd worked so hard for was ripped out from under me.

He still wanted me to come to his house, though. He was probably trying to get the team back together for the tournament at the end of the week. But if he couldn't play, there was no way I was going to just walk in and lose like that.

"It's a brutal situation," Ryker said, bringing a knee to the floor to stop his push-ups.

"Right," I said. "It's like the worst possible situation ever. It's like I've been playing my guts out, but I messed everything up." I shook my head. My brain was still screaming about it all. It had felt good to do some pull-ups in the doorway, but it hadn't released all the explosion inside.

My brother nodded. Then he did this obnoxious thing and didn't say anything through his next reps. Maybe he was thinking of what to say, or was just hoping I'd calm down. I did more pull-ups while I waited.

After his set, he sat up again. "You've still got a choice," he said, his arms over his knees, a little sweat on his forehead.

Great. Here it came. I dropped down off the pull-up bar to face him.

"You have to decide whether the game is over or not."

"What?" I asked.

"Is the game over?" he repeated. "Let's say a player is in a tough game, and trying really hard. The opposition is brutal, and his teammates are definitely not perfect. But he made some mistakes. Maybe even some terrible ones." I didn't like where this was going. "Maybe he's even afraid that what he did might cost him the game, and ruin things with his teammates." He paused. "If the game is over, then what?"

I shrugged. "He blew it," I said, feeling the words. I knew I had messed it up, like game-on-the-line-in-the-playoffs messed up. This talk definitely wasn't helping. "He owns up to his team," I said, hating the words. Coaches had drilled that one into my head. You had to own your mistakes, but I definitely didn't want to do that in this case. Even picturing having to face Edelle in real life was hard. "Then he goes home and probably can't stop thinking about how he messed up, or how other people didn't do their part and that made him mess up, and if there's any way he could have done better." That was going to be my life.

"Right," Ryker said, standing to stretch, "but what if there are still five minutes on the clock? Does that change things?"

"Maybe," I said, looking at my brother. "Then he's got time."

My brother nodded. "What would you want someone who messed up to do if there were five minutes on the clock?"

I looked at him, something turning inside me. "Go in there and give it all he's got. Try to change everything. If he really goes after it, he could be a game-changer."

"Right," my brother said. "He still needs to own up to his team." He paused. "And I mean *really* own up." I still hated the idea of that. "But then he's got to play and play hard."

Whatever was turning inside me turned a little more.

"And," my brother said, "what happens if he plays really well? Like hold-nothing-back well?"

"It's a whole different game. He could be key in a huge comeback."

My brother nodded again. "A huge comeback," he repeated. "So you have to decide if this game is over, or if you have five minutes left." He crouched down to start another set of push-ups. "Personally, I think there's always time left. You can own up, and then I know what Hunter Athanasopoulos can do when the game is on the line."

CHAPTER 45

IN PERSON

Bradley

I looked down the sidewalk and saw Hunter waiting in front of Jasper's house, a sack in his hand.

And I was walking toward him.

As Bradley Horvath.

On purpose.

I had my mom drive past once to make sure it was Jasper's house, and that's when I saw Hunter. He was going to be there waiting for me. I also told my mom to drive up to the next street and drop me off. I kind of wanted the walk time to make sure I was ready for this.

And I wasn't sure I wanted my mom watching whatever happened.

I took a deep breath, and thought of all the other deep breaths I had taken this semester. I had been really brave, tried to reinvent myself, tried to be what I really wanted to be, reached out to people, danced, stood up for my friend . . . and it blew up on me. Like it ended terribly, like one of those movies that's moving toward an awesome end, but then your favorite character dies, and you develop trust issues.

But this was my movie, and I guess I was trying to make a better ending. At least giving it a shot. Or maybe I was just going to make it even worse, like everything else I did. Combustion, wreckage, tragedy, that sort of thing.

But maybe that wasn't entirely fair.

Maybe not everything I did exploded into a dumpster fire.

I had been invited places. I had danced in front of people, and I loved it. And they loved it. And I think I was kind of good at it. I texted people, and they texted back. I joined a team. Like a sports team. But also, kind of not like a sports team. But close enough that I felt really proud that I even tried.

And boy did I try.

I made friends. And I think they were real friends. I thought about Edelle at my doorstep with chocolates. I thought of Jasper and even Keiko.

But each step I took closer to Hunter made my stomach squeeze.

If I did all of those awesome things once as Daebak, maybe I could do them again . . . as Bradley.

Maybe even in my fat awkward body with regular brown hair and a basic junior high wardrobe. Maybe I could still do that stuff that I loved doing.

Maybe.

I forced myself to walk faster.

More deep breaths.

"Hey," I said, finally arriving.

This was the moment. Part of me really wanted to turn and run somewhere else, but I wasn't going to make "old Bradley" choices any more. And it was too late for that.

Hunter turned. It was kind of weird to see him in real life again. I had gotten used to his avatar. He seemed a little taller than last year, and had shaved part of his eyebrow. Probably something that the cool kids were doing lately. I don't know.

I could only see his face above his mask, but he scrunched his eyes against the sun. "Bradley Horvath?" A smile crossed his face. The same kind of smile when he was about to say something stupid.

"Yep," I said, the words coming out louder than I wanted. I guess talking louder was better than being too quiet. It was weird being recognized as my real self, but it also felt good.

I just stood there and waited.

"Wait," he said, "what are you doing h—?" He didn't finish his sentence, then his eyes got wider.

I nodded.

"No way," he said, his eyes growing big. "Daebak?"

I nodded. "Daebak." I tried not to sound too annoyed.

"Daebak was Bradley Horvath?" he said to himself, then he burst out laughing. "I never would have guessed."

"You didn't guess a lot of things," I said. I knew that would hurt a little. My heart thudded like there were horses galloping on my chest.

He stopped laughing.

I pointed at him. *"And* you were kind of a jerk." The words felt strange leaving my mouth.

He thought for a moment. "Oh, right . . ." he said, putting the pieces together, "the basketball hoop—"

"That wasn't cool," I said. "I don't know why you think you can treat people like that. Like the way you'd get mad at Vanya when she'd mess up in a game. Or ignoring people. Or trying to kick people off your team. You can't treat any of us like that."

He just stood there, thinking. I thought he would lash out and defend himself. Or make a joke or something, but he didn't. He said something I never expected Hunter to say. No matter how many times I ran through this conversation in my mind I'd never seen it going like this.

He bit his lip, and then he nodded and said, "You're right. You're totally right."

It took me off guard and I watched him, trying to decide if I believed him. "You made my life pretty miserable for years, teasing me with the whole 'Bradley peed his pants' thing."

It looked like he was going to say something, but then he stopped himself. Then he opened his mouth again. "Yeah," he said, "I didn't get it. It's not like I hated you or anything. I was just joking around."

"It wasn't funny to me." I paused as my emotions were getting bigger than I wanted them to, and I was *not* going to cry. It's just I remembered everything, the mocking, the loneliness. It bubbled up inside of me. "And what you did at the dance—"

"—was wrong," he interrupted, "and stupid." And then his confident conquer-the-world face got all squinched up for a second. "I messed up a lot of things. It was totally my fault. I was just worried about stuff, and trying to focus on something to help. And I didn't think . . ." He fumbled with his words. "I guess that doesn't matter. But I didn't know that Vanya was Edelle. And the more I think about it, the more I should have been like you, like the friend she had. And—" He stopped. "I'm no good at this. I'm just sorry."

I'm just sorry. I repeated his words in my head.

And I think he meant them.

I had planned on coming and saying my piece. I had planned on standing my ground and not letting Hunter laugh at me any-more. I had been ready for a confrontation. I had not planned on apologies. I was not ready to decide if I could forgive him. I was so off guard I just didn't know what to say.

"Don't ever throw anyone in a basketball hoop again," I said. It just kind of came out.

His mouth cracked into a hint of a smile, "I promise," he said.

It wasn't like we were friends now, but this was at least some-thing.

"And I was trying to think of something to help fix it all," Hunter said. "I didn't really know what, but . . ." Then he stopped. A van pulled up, Edelle in the passenger seat. "Looks like I'll just tell you all at once," Hunter said.

Edelle stepped out, but then the side door opened, and Keiko got out too. She looked surprisingly identical to her avatar.

And this was the first time she'd seen me in real life.

Not smooth Daebak, but Bradley, in all my glorious average-ness.

She looked at me.

"Hey, Keiko," I said. "I was Daebak, but my real name is Bradley."

She kept looking at me for a moment, then said, "Whatever."

And for the first time, I was glad to hear that tone, that total lack of emotion. She didn't seem to care at all if I was different.

"My real name is Keiko," she said, taking me off guard. "But my family calls me Kiki. If *you* call me Kiki, I will fill your bedroom with water balloons and fire ants." She rolled her eyes and stepped to the side.

Edelle smiled at me, then the smile disappeared as she looked at Hunter.

"Hey," he said.

She didn't say anything back.

"I've been a terrible friend," Hunter launched into an apology. "I had no idea you were Vanya. I just . . . I messed it up. And I didn't treat you like I should have. And it kind of felt like I was trapped, but . . ." He shook his head. "I shouldn't have said that. Bottom line is, I should have done better. No excuses."

"Good," Edelle said, "because I don't want to hear—" But she didn't finish her sentence. She cocked her head to the side and squinted, studying his face. "What's going on with your eyebrow?"

Hunter's mouth opened and closed as he seemed to be searching for words. "It's not an excuse for how I've acted," he said, "but I've been really worried about . . ." And then he took off his hat.

CHAPTER 46

SPOTS

Edelsabeth

"I'm balding," Hunter said. "It's probably temporary, at least I'm hoping it is. It's called alopecia." He turned his head and pointed at his hair. "Just in little sections, right now. Hopefully it will grow back."

I just stared. Sure enough, he had three spots on his head that were simply smooth skin, no curly blond hair at all.

That would be terrible. Plus, Hunter loved his hair. Every girl in Balderstein Middle loved his hair. I loved it.

"That's why I went to virtual school," he said. "To hide it. But that doesn't stop me from thinking about it every day. And that thinking about it got me all distracted, and I focused on all of the wrong things." He looked at me. "Like, I totally missed you."

"Um," I said, not really knowing how to respond.

"Wait," he said, "I'm not done. I messed up the dance and I'm trying to fix it. I was just about to tell Daeb . . . I mean, Horvath. I wrote an email to the administration and told them how sorry

I was. And I got an appointment and talked to Mila Holota, the lady over the whole school program. And I asked her if we could please do another dance." He looked at me. "I know you worked really hard on it, and I messed it all up. And I remembered how you wrote to the administration to get the dance changed in the first place, and I hoped it might work with my email too." .

He sent an email? He talked to Mila? He was trying to fix what he'd done. Sure, I was still upset that he didn't see me, that he wasn't the friend that I'd hoped he was, but this was a big step.

Then Hunter turned to Bradley. "And you seem to be really into that dance stuff. And I'll apologize to you at the dance in front of everyone," he said. "I'll even be one of those stupid fuzzy things and you can throw me in a hoop if you want."

Bradley smiled, then shook his head. "I'd probably miss."

Hunter smiled a little too. "You can still take a shot if you want."

"Pass," Bradley said. "I'm not really into humiliating people."

Hunter nodded. "You're a better man than me."

And then I hugged him. It just kind of happened. It wasn't like a best friend hug from before, but I did it. And then I hugged Bradley. Probably because I just hadn't hugged him yet.

"Ugh," Keiko said.

I let go of Hunter and looked at her.

"Don't even think about it," Keiko said.

Creaaak.

The front door to Jasper's house opened and he stepped out onto his front porch. "Everyone's here," he said, and lifted his arms. He looked exactly like his avatar. "And from what I saw out the window, you're all huggy." He smiled and pretended to hug us from far away.

We went and sat on his lawn facing the porch. We had to stay pretty far from him to keep him safe, but it was so good to see him. We talked about so many things. He asked us a lot of questions about school, and he saw Hunter's head and asked him questions too. And then we asked him about cystic fibrosis and how he was doing. He was recovering well, but still had to be careful.

"We brought you some gifts," I said. I had texted the idea to the others. I was pretty sure they brought stuff too.

"I didn't invite you here so you could bring me gifts," he said.

"But we did," I said.

He looked around. "Well then, we shouldn't waste them."

I had chocolates for him and a new video I had made from clips I had of him. Most of them were of his intense game face as we were practicing for the competition. He watched it and laughed.

Bradley texted Jasper a music gift card with some suggestions of his favorite songs. I think most of them were K-pop.

Keiko handed him a yellow gift bag with cute matching tissue paper sticking out of the top that she had brought. "Oh, this is epic!" Jasper said, reaching into the bag. He pulled out a teddy bear wearing a yellow tracksuit.

"I made it at the mall," Keiko said. "Push its belly."

Jasper used both thumbs to squeeze the bear's stomach.

"This is epic!" the bear said in Jasper's voice.

Jasper's eyes popped. "How did you do that?"

"Edelle helped me get a clip from your practices."

"That's amazing. Thank you," he said.

"Whatever," she said, but it was the first time I saw her totally and completely smile.

Hunter stood up with his paper grocery bag. "Mine is kind of dumb. Definitely not as cool as Keiko's bear." He reached into his bag and pulled out a foot-tall, two-columned trophy with a little lacrosse guy on the top. "I know you really wanted that tournament trophy, and this isn't even close. But maybe you could hold on to this one . . . I mean, until we see if we can pull off a miracle and get you the one you wanted." He smiled. "We probably don't have a shot at first or second, but maybe, if we really work hard the next few days, and we rock it, we can get third."

I realized what he was saying. "I thought you were quitting," I said.

"I was," he said. "I changed my mind. If you guys are still up for it."

I nodded.

Bradley did too.

"But I still can't play," Jasper said. "Not for at least a couple weeks. I'm really sorry, guys. My doctors would be so mad at me."

"Right," Hunter said, "but we'll still need you—and I have an idea about how you can help."

"Is it just going to be the three of us?" Bradley asked. "Any replacement can't be signed up for any other team."

There was an odd pause, and then everyone looked at Keiko.

"Ugh," she said.

CHAPTER 47

TOURNAMENT

Hunter

The stakes were high, we were in the middle of the tournament, I was trying to win Jasper a trophy, and I had a horde of alien insects trying to eat me for a snack.

Might as well be at the front.

I ran forward, spinning and shooting, hitting an alien beetle three times before it misted and I could focus on another spider.

Daebak and Vanya, or . . . Bradley and Edelle, whatever I was supposed to call them, hurried to help, firing and moving, dodging, and attacking. I could tell they were giving it their all, but they were nowhere as good as Jasper. He was still home recovering, and he couldn't play, but we needed him.

"Watch your left," Jasper called out. I whipped around to see a goopy alien scorpion only feet away. It took all my reflexes and speed to not be stung to death and still blast him.

"Epic!" Jasper yelled.

Jasper could join us in a spectator booth and call out

directions. We had to log onto his booth instead of the entire crowd of students watching, but it was worth it. He was our coach.

"Hunter, stay in the lead," Jasper said. "Edelle on the left, Daebak on the right."

Jasper filled in the hole in our team.

Edelle screamed, and I turned in time to see Daebak blast another monster. Once we planned better to cover for her after she screamed, she's done a lot better. Though the screams were still kind of funny.

"Keiko," Jasper said, "watch out. They're coming up behind you."

"Ugh," Keiko said, but then turned and blasted an alien mantis dead on, turning it to mist. She was actually a surprisingly good shot, but she never wanted to run. She liked to walk behind us.

It had taken a little bit to persuade her to join the team. But when Jasper asked, and Bradley told me to promise to drop off five packages of red licorice at her house to sweeten the deal, she gave in.

"Nice shot," Jasper said. "That alien mantis won't mess with Earth again." I could only imagine what his mother might be thinking with him yelling about alien mantises.

"Whatever," Keiko said.

"Three more coming down the left hall," Jasper said, "Move down the right; it will get you closer to the mother ship. Don't fight. Outrun them."

"I hate running," Keiko said.

We started moving down the hall, all in formation. This was

taking absolutely everything I had. Running and punching, twisting and dodging. Everyone was doing their best, but I was still trying to make up for Jasper.

And the truth was, the more I tried, the more I realized we didn't stand much of a chance to even get third place.

We scraped by in our first two events, with Jasper calling out orders. But we had seen our competition. And some of them were better than I thought.

But I couldn't give up—this was my five minutes left in the game.

"Millipede coming at you," Jasper said. His mom would think that was weird too. "And you guys are actually ahead of the other team. You've got this. You've got this," he said.

We might not win, but I wasn't giving up. Maybe this would be the comeback of the century. But if not, I think my teammates knew how hard I was trying, how I wanted to make up for how I'd messed up.

We'd see how long we could last.

And the longer we survived, the more Jasper would be yelling crazy things for his mom to hear.

CHAPTER 48

HEY, MOM

Edelsabeth

I had been editing for hours.

The video started off with me in one of my favorite shirts under my circle light. No filters.

"Hey, Mom," I said in the video, "I thought I'd put this video together to show you a few things."

The video cut to picture after picture of me last year from Instagram, and clips of videos from TikTok. Me with my puppy. Me hugging Kennedy. Me in my room. Me doing exercises. Me with the dinner Mom made. It even scrolled onto a picture of Parker's website and showed a few of the pictures of me I had saved.

My voice narrated, "I used to spend a lot of time thinking about what other people thought of me. And making myself look good," I said. "I was pretty good at it."

Then the screen went blank.

"Then you took all that away," my voice said. "You did it because you loved me, but I hated it."

Vanya appeared, walking around the VR school. "When I started recording for this video," I said, "I thought I was going to show you that I could *do* this, that I already knew everything about not caring too much about what I looked like. Like you were wrong, and I was right. Like I wasn't missing anything, didn't have any problems."

The view came back to me. "Well, I'm *not* going to say that I was wrong, and you were right." I pointed at the camera when I said the word *you.* "Because I don't think you need any encouragement."

I smirked. "But I did learn a few things."

Music came in, but not too loud, as the video launched into different footage. First Daebak. Him smiling. Him on *Skate-Coaster*. The two of us as little furry puffballs dancing.

"I learned that people love it when you get to know them."

Then Daebak was dancing, the camera cutting in when he whipped his hair, and panning out when he kicked out his foot and shifted his hips. "And when you don't spend your time trying to make yourself look good, but focus on someone else . . ." Daebak cocked his head and left arm to the side, then whirled into a 360 spin, " . . . you just might make a friend."

Vanya walked the halls again. "I learned what it's like to be glossed over or ignored. And to have a lot to offer, but other people not seeing it. Not giving you a chance."

"But others . . ." Jasper stacked huge blocks in *Creation*, then jumped on top of pillars in the obstacle course, then sat in his desk before science class smiling in his yellow jumpsuit. "Others will invite you to join in. And they won't let other people kick you out."

Keiko stood in the commons, no expression on her face. "And some people might never give you any encouragement, but they still might really, *really* need to receive it."

Hunter, the virtual version, put up his glowing fists, ready to blast aliens. "And some people make big mistakes, but can also have an amazing comeback."

The video cut back to Daebak again, laughing after he tripped a little in one of his dances. He looked down at the camera, dancing again, then covered his face. "I've learned that some people you used to ignore may be absolutely incredible. And they might give you a second chance too."

Then I cut back to me.

"And I learned that *being* good is a lot more important than *looking* good." I took a deep breath. "I know, it sounds like a fridge magnet, but it's true."

Me. No filter. Smiling.

"There it is, Mom," I said. "You were right." I blew my hair out of my eyes. "Don't let it go to your head."

CHAPTER 49

NOT BAD

Bradley

I sat there looking at my phone.

Don't judge me.

Summer was completely dead, and I was in mourning.

But I wasn't eating Kix in my dad's recliner—I did that earlier this morning.

I sat alone on the hard plastic bench in the commons of the real Balderstein Junior High, staring at pic after pic on my phone. They were all in a jumbled order:

—Edelle's little sister with a chocolate face.

—An amazing picture of a giraffe made from different colored thumbtacks pushed into a board.

—A small, impressive turtle made from cardboard.

(Those last two were Keiko's. Turns out she's quite the artist.)

—Edelle was showing off a scarf made by some girl she met that I didn't know.

—Daebak making the weirdest face, light bursting from his

fist at an alien beetle, and Vanya about to get eaten in the background.

—Jasper coming back to school to play with us again for the first time.

—All the members of JaVaHuDaKe receiving fourth-place trophies. (Edelle's mom had sent an email to the administration explaining Jasper's illness, and how hard the team had tried with very little time to help Keiko learn, and how they still came together to get fourth. They decided to make trophies just for us.)

—Keiko, not smiling, standing on the sideline at Hunter's lacrosse game. (If you look really closely, in the background you can see Ruby and Grace, but they look nothing like their avatars.)

Edelle's mom let her back on social media, with some limits. And I liked looking at her pics. Some of it was her family, some of it was awesome stuff about other people she knew, and some of it was like my history.

"Bradley."

I looked up, and immediately knew who it was.

"Hey," I said, standing up, "you wore it."

"Of course," he said, "and it looks epic." Jasper stretched out his arms to give a full view of his bright yellow tracksuit. Not teddy bear sized—Jasper sized. We'd all pitched in and got it for his birthday. Jasper and his parents decided that he was doing well enough to come to school in person, but he would only attend half days to begin with.

"You look good too," he said.

It was just me, Bradley Horvath. No avatar this time.

"Thanks," I said. I was wearing jeans, an Avalanche hat Jasper got me for Christmas, a Bubble Girls T-shirt Keiko got me, and the leather jacket Edelle and I had found at a secondhand store and then attached a whole string of little dangly things down both arms.

"I didn't think we could wear hats," Jasper said.

"We can't," I said. "I'll take it off when the bell rings."

"Keiko!" Jasper called out and spread his arms to hug her. She didn't move. "Can I hug you?" he asked.

"Whatever," she said, flatly. But as he wrapped his arms around her, a crack of a smile definitely came out.

And then I was getting a hug too, but from someone else. I think I blushed almost every time it happened. Even though she didn't wear as much makeup and fancy clothes as she used to, I never thought I'd start off the year by getting hugged by a girl like her in the commons of the school.

I never would have guessed.

Not in a billion years.

"Two thousand five hundred and thirty-one views!" Edelle said, lifting her arms in celebration.

I smiled pretty big.

About halfway through last year, Edelle had persuaded me to start releasing my Daebak dance videos on social media outside the school. They got some traction and I got quite a few likes. But when the summer started, she convinced me to rebrand. To start new.

To just be me—Bradley.

That decision took a lot of deep breaths. But it was really working. I was connecting with all sorts of people, and views were growing every day. Who knew people might like watching this big guy move to the music? I even had this dancer from the local college duet me, and a boy about my same size say that because of me, he was going to start posting his videos too.

"You did most of the work," I told Edelle. She was even better working with real life shots than virtual ones, like filming me dancing in front of the state capitol building, or under a streetlight, or in front of an old train.

Then Jasper started to beatbox. That was a signal, one of his favorite things to do now to challenge me. He wasn't professional at it or anything; he was just trying to give me a beat. There, in front of the huge big glass doors of the school, all the new students coming in, he was trying to get me to dance.

So I did.

That's right, big Bradley Horvath started to dance in the middle of the lobby at his new junior high.

Not Daebak—Bradley.

Jasper and Edelle clapped and cheered while I kept going, shifting to the left, then doing this stutter-then-turn I had been working on. (That got a rise out of them.) Keiko clapped just after everyone else, giving it a cool syncopated feel. A few people I didn't know walked by and clapped and cheered me on. A few others even laughed a little. But I didn't care. (It's amazing how having a few people cheering for you makes it easier not to worry about the others that aren't.)

I had just stopped dancing and high-fiving my friends when a booming voice rang through the school. "What's up, people?" Hunter Athanasopoulos walked through the front doors and started giving people high fives. "Let's get this going," he said, and clapped several times.

His golden locks were gone. He had short hair now. He'd developed one more bald spot before they'd started filling back in. He had his hair buzzed so it could all grow back together.

In the end, I'd really liked virtual school, and I might have even stayed another year. Except I got outvoted. Everyone else wanted to go back.

And so I did it.

In a way, it was kind of like starting as a new me again. I mean, I was still Bradley Horvath, but I got invited to things, and I had friends.

And sometimes I had the confidence to dance.

"Whoa," Hunter said, finally making it over to our group, "you can't wear a hat to school," he said, staring at me. "I should know." He rubbed his hand over his short hair.

I nodded and took it off. I wasn't really waiting for the bell, just for all my friends to be there.

Edelle smiled huge.

"Epic," Jasper said.

Hunter shrugged. "It's cool if you like it."

"Not bad," Keiko said and nodded a little.

And I ran my fingers through my bright pink hair.

Discussion Questions

1. What was your experience with school during the pandemic? Were you like Bradley, who loved doing online school? Or were you more like Edelle or Hunter, who really struggled with it? Why? What was good and what was bad about it for you?

2. If you had the chance to try virtual school, would you want to? Why or why not?

3. Bradley wanted to look different and start over. Why might that be appealing? Why might it be scary?

4. Edelle's mom wanted her to become less concerned about how she looked. Why might being too focused on physical appearance be a problem with some people today? Why might it be nice to be less concerned with how we look?

5. Would you want to form a team and do the virtual game challenge? Why or why not? Who would you want to be on your team? Which game do you think you'd be best at?

6. If you could choose your own avatar, what would it look like? Would it look more or less like you right now?

7. Keiko was initially reluctant to go to the dance. Are you usually outgoing, or do you need convincing to spend time with lots of other people? How is being outgoing a good thing, and how is it a bad thing?

8. Jasper had some physical challenges that made it hard for him to compete in sports. If there was something you liked to do that you weren't able to for any reason, how would you react?

9. Hunter made some big mistakes and had to work really hard to try to make them right. Why do you think it's important to try to make things right when we make a mistake?

10. Bradley, Hunter, and Edelle all made changes in their lives based on their experiences in virtual school. Who do you feel is closest to your experiences at school? Have your experiences in school or with your friends changed you?

Acknowledgments

Thanks time!

Thanks so much for reading this book. We love it when anyone gives our stories a chance. Without readers there are no books. We'd love to hear what you thought. Feel free to reach out to us on social media or write us at chadcmorris@gmail.com. If you liked *Virtually Me*, please tell others about it. You also might look into our other books, *Willa and the Whale*, *Squint*, *Mustaches for Maddie*, the Cragbridge Hall trilogy, and *Ghostsitter*.

We are so grateful to the Shadow Mountain Publishing team. The first draft of this book was based on a great idea and had a lot of fun elements, but it was rough. Like needs-an-overhaul rough. Thanks to Chris Schoebinger, Lisa Mangum, and Heidi Taylor for their frank feedback, patience, and belief in us. We're very thankful for the help and guidance. We rewrote the book and loved how it turned out.

Thanks to Derk Koldewyn for his work and editorial polish.

He made our writing better. Thanks to Garth Bruner for the artwork for the cover and the memes. Thanks to Richard Erickson for the art direction, and Rachael Ward for typesetting. Thanks for using your talents! And thanks to our sensitivity readers and their feedback.

Thanks to Ben Grange for his great work and support as our agent. And thanks to Josh Hale and Abi Tregaskis for being youth readers and giving us feedback. Thanks!